T

by

Patrick D. Gallaher

**THE BLACK DEMON**

Copyright © 2015 Patrick D. Gallaher

All Rights Reserved.

ISBN-13:9781511469791

# Prologue

The young woman moved with the athletic grace of a mermaid beneath the red keel of the yacht as she swam toward the stern. Her blue eyes were opened and her long red hair flowed over her back as she carefully maneuvered underneath the large propeller blades.

She was only twenty-one years old. Her only pocessions were a black bag that was strapped over her shoulder like a purse, two diver fins on her feet and a red bikini that revealed her slim, tanned body.

The young woman was not in the least bit worried as she swam beneath the ship's keel. This area had a large population of sharks, but she had swam with them before and had never been attacked once. The only predators that concerned her at the moment were above the surface on the decks of the two ships, waiting for her.

The woman came out from under the stern and surfaced in front of the ladder on the deck. She had expected to see her father standing there waiting to help her out of the water. Instead, she saw exactly who she did not want to see. An unshaven man with a scar running down the right side of his face looked down at her with his arms folded.

"Is it done?" the man asked in Russian.

"Where is my father?" the woman said in her native language.

"Is it done?!" the man repeated.

She nodded. "Yes. It's done."

"Good."

The man reached down and grabbed her by the hair. The woman screamed as he pulled her onto the deck and she saw her worst fear coming true. She demanded, pleaded for him to stop as he slapped her across the face, knocking her to the floor. As the scarred man pulled her to her feet once more, the young woman called out for her father.

"Papa! Papa!"

She saw him on the stern of the other ship with the captain, his head bowed in sorry as he tried to ignore her pleas. As she was dragged inside, the young woman had a look of complete disbelief and hopelessness as she realized that she was on her own.

The captain of the other vessel put his hand on the father's shoulder. "It's a necassary sacrifice for the Motherland, Comrade."

The woman continued to struggle against the scarred man as he dragged her downstairs into the engine room. He finally let her go then backhanded her across the face again, knocking her to the floor. He then grabbed both of her hands, took out a pair of handcuffs and chained her arms high above her head to a metal steam pipe.

Without saying another word, the scarred man walked out of the room. He ignored the young woman's cries for help as he walked back out onto the stern and boarded his own vessel with his fellow comrades.

As soon as he was on board the spy ship pulled away closer to the island where the crew would watch the yacht go down once the scuttling charge that the woman had attached to the keel was set off. The six-man crew all stood on the bridge as the captain held up the detonation control. The young woman's father closed his eyes as the captain pressed the button, not wishing to see his daughter dragged down to her death.

They never knew what hit them.

The spy ship was ripped in-half in a terrific blast that blew its guts out.

In the engine room of the yacht, as she sat alone with her hands held high above her head unable to move, Natalia Ravoc heard the explosion outside and sobbed as she realized that she had just killed the last member of her family.

# 1

The small port village of Puerto Villamil is located on the southeastern edge of the island of Isla Isabele in the Galapagos Islands. It is one of the largest human settlements in the archipelago; most of the two-thousand plus citizens living on the island reside in this small town, making their living by either fishing or from the yearly tourists that visit the area. Puerto Villamil is also a popular stop for private yachts and on this night the harbor was packed with sailboats.

On the beach a young woman in a dark bathing suit ran down to the dock, smiling and laughing as she looked over her shoulder at her pursuing boyfriend. She ran barefoot almost down to the end of the dock, finally stopping and allowing him to catch up to her. The young lady smiled as the man walked up in front of her, took her in his arms and kissed her full on the mouth. He cupped her soft face in his hands and looked into her deep beautiful eyes.

"I love you," he told her.

"I love you," she replied.

They both stood for a moment staring out toward the sea, then they embraced on the front of the dock.

Off in the distance, unnoticed by the loving couple, a line of sailboats tied up to buoys in the middle of the harbor began to move. The sailboat farthest out moved first, its mast slowly rocking back and forth as an unseen mass glided silently beneath its keel. Then the next sailboat in line began to sway from side-to-side as well, and then a third. Before long the entire row of sailboats was moving back and forth in the wake of the enormous object moving beneath them into the harbor.

The woman kissed her boyfriend a final time, her back facing out toward the ocean. She leaned back and smiled. "How would you like to go for a swim?"

Suddenly the ocean behind her exploded as a large girth launched itself out of the water and onto the dock. The woman screamed as the wooden floor between them suddenly broke in-two, the front end that she was on falling at an angle into the water with a loud splash. Her boyfriend grabbed onto her hands as she fell, catching her before she could slide down. The woman turned her head to see what had attacked them and saw a horrifying sight.

A giant great white shark as big as a whale hyperextended its upper jaw of white triangular teeth as it fought to reach its prey on the severed dock. The shark had a dark black coloriation on its upper body and huge black lifeless eyes.

The woman screamed again as the enormous monster snapped its jaws up at her. She turned over onto her back as her boyfriend fought to pull her to safety, her bare feet kicking against the animal's conical snout as it continued to snap at her. The man yelled at his girfriend to hold onto him as he tried to pull her up, but she was making so much movement that he was starting to lose his grip on her.

The terrified woman kicked frantically as she began to slide down toward the shark's murderous teeth that opened and closed in horrifying snaps. As she struggled, she crept closer and closer to the shark's mouth and she knew that she was only seconds away from an agonizing death that she could not imagine.

Realizing that her end was near the young woman cried out, "Please God, help me."

Then, as if in answer to her prayer, the shark stopped. It became completely still as if it had suddenly died. The man quickly pulled his lover up onto the dock. As the terrified couple watched the giant shark slid backwards into the water and disappeared. The woman began to cry, burying her face into the man's chest as he tried to comfort her.

Below the surface, the shark moved silently through the water as its crescent tail propelled it with short sweeps back out into the ocean. Its mouth remained opened just enough to allow a rush of water through its gills. As it made its way back out to deep water, it was suddenly joined by a six-foot long, propeller-driven vessel that seemed to resemble a shark itself. A small bulb on top of the torpedo-shaped object flashed light every five seconds as it turned below the water's surface out toward a research vessel in the open ocean.

As if hypnotized by the strange unmanned machine, the shark followed.

On the bridge of the 195-foot long United States Naval Research yacht *Squalas*, a man with a thick scraggly beard and wire-rimmed glasses sat staring at a laptop computer, his hand turning a small joystick as he guided both the unmanned submersible and the giant shark back out to sea.

# 2

The gray Jeep Wrangler pulled up to the main gate at Pearl Harbor, Hawaii. The driver slowed to a stop as a uniformed guard came out of the office. Jason Shaw pulled out his driver's license and his identification papers for the guard to look over. After signing the visitors' logbook, the marine then waved him through.

Jason pulled up and parked in front of a large concrete building near the dock area. He turned off the ignition and stepped out onto the parking lot just as a red convertible pulled up alongside. Harry Jacobs was about six inches shorter than Jason at five feet, nine inches, with a rough beard, wire-rimmed glasses and a ridiculous red cap that seemed to match his car.

"Hey, Harry," said Jason. "What's with the hat?"

Harry did his best to ignore Jason's insult as they walked alongside each other toward the entrance of the building. He was not in the mood for his co-worker's sarcasm. As if having to explain to the boss how their test subject had escaped wasn't bad enough he also had to put up with Jason's bullspit attitude as well.

"It was a gift from my mother," he said.

"Well, whatever you do don't wear it to your next job interview."

"Shut up."

Both men passed through the entrance and stepped up to a desk where a lovely blonde-haired lady in a white navy uniform looked up at them from her computer.

"Good morning," Jason said with a smile. "Doctors Shaw and Jacobs are here to see Admiral Zanuck."

The woman typed at her computer for a moment, then looked back at the two men. "Aw, yes. The Admiral is expecting you."

Harry and Jason walked to the elevator across the room and pressed the button to go up to the tenth floor. When the door opened they stepped inside, Harry doing his best in his aggravated annoyance to avoid talking to the taller man standing next to him as they ascended.

Harry Jacobs and Jason Shaw were not the best of friends. They had met four years earlier when both of them had graduated from college at the top of their class and were hired as navy scientests on a top secret project to use marine animals under their control to conduct dangerous underwater missions for the navy. The official name of the operation was: PROJECT SEA REX.

For a while, both men seemed to work very well together but after Harry began dating Jason's sister Sarah a year earlier Jason started to become more competitive toward his partner. He liked to get him rialed up and pushed his buttons in every way that he could. Harry was not sure if he was just being protective of his little sister or if he had just been pocessed by an evil little troll. Either way, Jason's rude and sarcastic attitude had made Harry dread coming back to work after every weekend for the past year. The fact of the matter was that Harry was also spoiled, with everything having been provided for him his entire life and unable to take a joke.

He was also not thrilled that Jason had been given a higher position by Admiral Zanuck in Project Sea Rex, which nearly made Jason his boss. The reason for that, however, was the fact that Jason had been more dedicated to the project than Harry had been, doing practically all of the designs by himself.

After a few moments the elevator finally came to a stop. Jason leaned down toward Harry and said quitely, "Remember, mind your mannerisms."

Harry took a deep breath to ease his blood pressure as the elevator doors opened and they both walked down the hall to a door with two guards standing outside.

After showing the guards their identity cards one of them opened the door for Harry and Jason, revealing a large room inside with pictures of famous naval battles on the wall. The entire back wall was a large glass window that gave a spectacular view of Pearl Harbor and Ford Island. The leather chair behind the desk turned around and the man seated in it eyed the two navy doctors with a clear look of disapproval.

Admiral Carl Zanuck stared at the two doctors as they came into his office. He was dressed in his crisp white Navy admiral's uniform. His graying hair was comed back and his towering six-foot frame was evident as he sat up straight in his seat.

Zanuck was the one who had assigned Harry and Jason to Project Sea Rex four years earlier and had become impressed by the work that they had accomplished since then. But as Harry and Jason sat down in their own chairs they could both sense that their boss was anything but thrilled.

The Admiral tossed a newspaper onto his desk for the two civilians to look at. Jason read the headline:

# GIANT SHARK TERRORIZES GALAPAGOS

"I certainly hope that one of you can explain this to me," said Zanuck with a gravelly voice. "You gentlemen have been given the best technology available for this project. How is it that a sixty-foot great white shark under your control manages to slip out of its cage and swim three-thousand miles out before you can use your mind-control device to regain control of it?"

Harry had been nervous about having this meeting since he was told to report to Admiral Zanuck's office upon returning in the navy yacht with the shark that morning.

Jason on the other hand kept his cool. "That's a good question, Admiral. Harry?"

Harry suddenly realized that Jason and the Admiral were both staring at him, waiting for him to answer. It was obvious that Jason was just trying to make him look bad in front of the Admiral. But on the other hand securing the giant shark's aquatic pen was his responsibility.

"The shark broke out of its cage at around 0200 hours on June 20," Harry began. "I was informed by one of the staff at the aquatic facality shortly afterwards and ordered the *Squalas* to be made ready to set sail immediatly. By the time I got underway the shark was already a hundred miles out to sea."

"How did you find out where it was heading?" asked Zanuck.

"We had a tracking device implanted in the animal for just a situation like this."

Zanuck massaged his temple as he considered the next question. "So you were able to track this thing across the Pacific but you weren't able to regain control of it until it almost killed two people in the Galapagos Islands?"

Harry nodded. "Yes, sir."

"Why the hell not?"

"Because Bruce is just a prototype, sir," Jason intervened. "He's only a test subject."

"Bruce?" Zanuck asked, confused.

"Yes, sir. That's the name we gave the shark. As I was saying, the neural implant that we placed in its brain can only allow us to control him from a radius of a hundred yards and even that can only be done with a remote submersible to guide him."

Zanuck leaned back in his chair and looked at the two scientests. "Do you both realize what I had to go through to cover up this event? You're just very lucky that no one was killed. This incident, no matter how big or small, is one incident too many. You gentlemen have been given the opportunity to have complete control over what is now the most dangerous animal on the planet. I suggest that you keep a tighter leash on it. Because if anything like this happens again I will see to it that Project Sea Rex is terminated. And I don't care what new breakthroughs that you may have made. Do I make myself clear?"

Harry and Jason nodded and quietly said, "Yes, sir."

"On the brighter side, Doctor Jacobs," the Admiral continued, "the fact that you were able to guide that thing all the way back to its pen from across the ocean is nothing short of impressive. Your team has come a long way since you first started this project."

Harry felt slightly relieved at the Admiral's compliment. "Thank you, sir."

"Thank you for coming in, gentlemen," Zanuck said. "That will be all for now."

Harry and Jason stood with their commanding officer and shook hands before leaving the office.

After returning to the elevator Jason said, "That went well. He is right, though. You did do a bang up job in bringing our lives' work back to its cage."

Harry wasn't sure if Jason was really complementing him or if he was somehow teasing him once more. He decided not to ask which. "So what do you want to do now?" he asked, changing the subject.

Jason checked the time on his cell phone.

"Let's fly over to the *Garage Sale*. I need to go check up on Bruce."

# 3

The giant shark moved silently through the water of its open ocean prison, its six-foot dark-colored dorsal fin knifing across the surface. Its crescent tail made short sweeps as it slowly swam around the interior of metal bars, looking for a way out. The damage that it had been able to exploit and escape through two weeks before had been repaired. At the moment, this massive predator had a will of its own as it swam through its watery domain. But once its owners activated the neural implant installed into the top of its brain, this massive leviathan would become an underwater drone, totally obediant to its master controlling it from above the surface. And so the sixty-foot shark known as "Bruce" was once again doomed to swim forever in its open ocean prison with no hope of ever being free, or independent.

The floating facality that was the shark's aquatic cage sat in a secure remote area off the Hawaiian Coast where only U.S. naval vessels were allowed to sail. From the surface, with the naval yacht *Squalas* tied up to the pier, it looked mostly like a floating dock equipped with a large square metal walkpath and a small facality on the northeast corner. But the real facalities were beneath the surface.

This floating assylum had originally been built for training purposes by the U.S. Navy. After Admiral Zanuck gained control of it to be used as the headquarters for Project Sea Rex it was refitted with a large aquatic pen and an underwater lab. It was also equipped with underwater living quarters for the staff. Because the Navy had never actually given the top secret floating facality an official identity, Jason had decided to give it his own code name: *SS Garage Sale*.

Harry Jacobs stood on the northeast corner of the facality in a blue-and-black diver's wetsuit as he examined a tablet of inspections that he was completing on the shark's cage. Every now and then his eyes would turn up to look over his wire-rimmed glasses at the shark's black dorsal fin knifing across the surface, making sure that Bruce stayed a safe distance away from him while he finished his work. Upon looking down the east walkpath of the facality, Harry soon found himself distracted by something more promising.

Walking toward him was a young woman dressed in a casual white T-shirt and small blue jeans short shorts, which revealed a pair of tanned slender legs. Around her neck was an identification card attached to a necklace. She wore red slippers on her feet. Her blonde hair seemed to reflect the sunlight like gold and a pair of sunglasses shielded her violet eyes.

Sarah Shaw possessed an air of confidence in her white-toothed smile, and yet underneath her beauty one could also sense a spoiled brat.

She removed her glasses as she approached Harry, putting her arms around his neck and kissing him softly on the mouth. At five feet, six inches, she was about the same height as he was.

"Morning, Sunshine," said Sarah as she leaned back in his arms. "Did you miss me?"

Harry pulled her in close once more until their foreheads touched. "You have no idea. Your brother has been getting on my last nerve as usual."

Sarah eased his suffering by giving him that wicked smile that he had always loved from her. "Stay the course, my love," she whispered. "Our day of reckoning is close at hand now. I can feel it."

Harry moved his hand beneath her shirt and gently rubbed the smooth skin of her back. "Funny," he said. "I can feel something as well."

Their lips were about to come together once again when the shark suddenly surfaced right next to them. Sarah screamed in surprise and backed up into Harry's embrace as Bruce's conical snout and terrifying teeth emerged right next to the walkpath, its black lifeless eye looking at them as it turned and whipped its crescent tail into the air before vanishing beneath the surface.

Harry and Sarah both stared in shock at the churning water where Bruce had scared them for a moment. Then they both looked up the walkpath, where Jason stood holding a laptop computer in his hands.

"The shark is working!" Jason laughed.

Sarah rolled her eyes at her brother. She walked up to him with the intention of slapping him while Harry decided to stay back and let the two siblings have their confrontation.

"Dammit Jason," Sarah yelled. "You scared the hell out of me. Are you proud of yourself?"

Jason smiled at his sister's rage as he closed the laptop. "Very proud."

"Jason, that wasn't funny. I saw my whole life flash before my eyes. Is this really the kind of welcome that my older brother has waiting for me every time that I come to visit?"

Jason's first thought was to say something sarcastic, but the words never left his mouth. He now had to admit that using Bruce for one of his pranks was irresponsible. "You're right," he said finally. "I'm sorry. That is no way to welcome your family as they walk in. And I am glad to see you. Hug?"

Sarah stood there for a moment with her hands on her hips. Slowly, her frown turned into a soft smile and she walked forward and hugged him. Jason wrapped his muscled arms around his sister's slender body and lifted her up in a loving embrace. Sarah's small figure was dwarfed by Jason's robust form as he held her.

After a moment he finally put her down and kissed her on the cheek. "So what brings you to the *Garage Sale?*"

"Well," said Sarah, "I came to invite you and Harry to the firework show tonight at Honolulu. It's the Fourth of July, you know?"

Jason gave her a disappointed look as he opened his computer again. "I'm so sorry, Sarah. I hate to say no but some friends of mine have already invited me to join them at their own party tonight."

"Oh?" said Sarah, trying to look disappointed. "And where is that going to be?"

"Just off Hovana Point. We're going to be watching fireworks on my friend's yacht from out at sea." Jason looked at his sister for a moment as she seemed lost in thought. "You're not mad, are you?"

Sarah shook her head. "No. I was just inviting you to have a good time, that's all. But it sounds like you've already got your own plans."

That's a first, Jason thought. He couldn't even remember the last time that his sister had ever wanted anything to do with him. Ever since they were kids Sarah had always acted like Jason was annoying her just by walking into the room and she often enjoyed using harsh talk that was meant to hurt him and make him feel like a fool. But what Jason had really come to hate about his sister was that fake smile that she often produced that said "drop dead" behind it.

He remembered last year when his father had invited him to a family Thanksgiving party at their grandparents' house. "Your sister is going to be there," his father had said on the telephone. "I'm sure that she would like to see you."

Jason laughed at that. "I can't remember the last time that Sarah *ever* wanted to see me, Dad."

Jason often wondered if he had done something to make her act the way that she did. At some point he had given up trying to make friends with his sister and instead decided to try and stay away from her and out of her way, figuring that's what she wanted. The fact that she was wanting to spend time with him now was something very unusual for her.

Maybe he should have been suspicious.

"I promise we'll get together on the next July 4th," Jason told her.

Sarah shrugged. "Okay. Maybe next year then."

Jason smiled as he put his hand on his sister's shoulder and kissed her gently on the cheek. "I gotta get back to work. I'll see you next week. I love you."

"Love you, too."

Sarah stood there with her arms folded as she watched him walk away. She was actually glad that Jason had turned down her invitation. Now that she knew where he was going to be tonight there would never be a better opportunity than now. She couldn't help but smile slightly as she saw her plans that she had been preparing for the past two years finally coming together.

She turned her head to look at Bruce's black dorsal fin as it cut through the water of its submerged prison.

"Happy Fourth of July, brother."

# 4

Sarah emerged from the shower of her Honolulu apartment dressed in a white bath robe. She sat down in front of her bedroom mirror and began combing her hair. There was a knock at the door.

"Come In."

The door opened and Harry Jacobs walked inside. Sarah smiled at his reflection as he walked up to her and kissed her on the cheek.

"You said on the phone that you had something urgent to talk to me about. What's wrong?"

"Nothing's wrong," said Sarah. "Actually, everything is perfect." She turned around in her chair and then stood up to face him. "It needs to be done tonight. Jason will be on a sailboat with friends on the open ocean. That will be the perfect time for you to use Bruce to tie up loose ends for us."

Harry placed his hands on her back and gently pressed her body aganist his, feeling uneasy about what they were both planning. "Sarah, is this really necessary? I mean, I know that your father's will promised Jason a bigger share of his fortune than he did for you but you're still getting ten million dollars. It's not like you need Jason's money."

Sarah wrapped her arms around his neck and kissed him softly on the mouth. "I don't care if I don't need it. I want it. Harry, sweetie. If you're too nervous to go through with this just tell me."

Harry shook his head. "I'm just new to this sort of thing. That's all. Besides, it's not like I'll miss him. Jason has made my life miserable since the day you and I first started dating. I'll be more than happy to have him out of my life."

Sarah made a slight grin and pressed her forehead against his.

"Our lives."

# 5

The Pacific Ocean around the lone sailboat was flat calm as the small vessel floated a few miles off the northern tip of Oahu. The name on the stern in light blue letters read *AMITY*. The four young people on board-two men, two women-watched the display of fireworks that lit up the night sky along the Hawaiian coastline.

Jason was enjoying himself more than he thought he would be. The blind date that his friend Ben had for him, a long-haired blonde named Susan, had turned out to be better than Jason had thought she would be. Not only was she fun to be around, she was also beautiful. She wore an American flag bikini bra and cut blue jean shorts that revealed a lovely curved body and a silver piercing in her belly button. Not exactly the kind of wear that Jason would have expected from a blind date, but he wasn't about to complain.

Susan sat down on the boat's stern next to Jason as they made casual conversations, getting to know each other. Their feet dangled over the side above the water. Ben and his girlfriend had gone inside to get some drinks, leaving Jason and Susan to get more aquainted.

"So how long are you going to be in Hawaii?" asked Susan.

Jason smiled. "Actually, I work here. I'm a civilian scientest in the US Navy."

"Really? What kind of work do you do?"

"The kind I'm not suppose to talk about."

"Oh. Top secret stuff, huh?" When Jason offered nothing more she prodded at him for more information. "Can you at least give me a hint?"

Jason smiled again. "I don't know you that well, honey. We just met."

Susan raised her hand. "Okay, okay. Say no more."

They both laughed at her attempt to change the subject and watched another spectacular display of fireworks illuminate the beach several miles away.

Susan looked over at Jason. "I'm really having a great time tonight."

Jason grinned as he slid his hand onto hers. "Yeah," he said. "Me, too."

Jason had to admit that he was having a better time on this Fourth of July night than he had had in a while. Susan was the first woman he had talked to in almost a year that had been able to make him smile. Finding a date for Jason was not difficult; he was handsome, polite and successful in life, but he quickly found that none of the women he met were interested in a serious relationship and many even had the same spoiled, harsh attitude as his sister. Finding a woman who was considerate, understanding and honest had proven to be difficult for Jason.

He blamed part of that reason on his commitment to his job. Jason had dedicated much of his time over the past years to his work on Project Sea Rex and had left little space for family and friends. Although his commitment to his duties was what made Admiral Zanuck promote him to chief engineer on the project, his hard work had largely prevented him from pursuing a successful love life.

Now, for the first time in months, he felt relaxed as he sat on a boat on the open ocean, accompanied by good friends and a gorgeous blonde that he really liked, plenty of drinks to keep the party going all night, and fireworks lighting up the sky in the distance.

He couldn't help but notice also how unusually calm the water was. Not a single wave rocked the *Amity* as it sat on the pond-like surface. The conditions were perfect for this occasion.

Jason felt so good in that moment as he sat next to Susan drinking his beer that he was almost certain that something was about to go wrong.

In the pitch black darkness beneath the sailboat, the shark-shaped underwater drone moved silently under the *Amity's* keel. And somewhere in the darkness Bruce homed in on the remote sub. The giant shark did not have a will of its own.

Less than a thousand yards away, Harry and Sarah sat inside their own sailboat. Harry was guiding the shark with his laptop computer, which was transmitting a signal through the mini-sub and into the shark's neural implant. At that moment, Harry was in complete control of Bruce's mind.

Jason had worked endlessly on this project from the beginning, finding a way to control the mind of the giant shark that they had created through genetic engineering in order to increase its overall length to five times its normal size.

Thanks to his partner's detailed knowledge and instructions, Harry now knew all of the ins and outs of the entire project to the point where he would be able to build it all over again by himself if he needed to. Now he was going to kill his partner with the very beast that they had created together.

As Sarah stood behind him, hugging his shoulders and staring at the computer screen, Harry ordered the shark to go deep.

Bruce pointed his nose down and swept his tail furiously as he dove into the darkness below. Then he reappeared, jaws agape, his upper gums exposing a murderous row of triangular teeth. Shooting up from below, Bruce slammed into the keel of the *Amity* like a locomotive.

The impact from below caught the four people on the *Amity* completely off guard, lifting the sailboat out of the water and causing Jason and Susan to fly across the deck. Jason managed to grab onto the metal railing just before falling into the water.

Susan fell backwards into the Pacific.

Jason quickly pulled himself back onto the deck as Susan resurfaced. "Susan, are you okay?"

"What was that?" Susan yelled, terrified.

Jason reached out to pull her back on board. Their hands had just touched when Susan was suddenly lifted out of the water from underneath.

Jason watched in horror as Susan rose thirty feet into the air in the giant shark's mouth. She screamed in terror as rows of razor sharp teeth crushed her torso in its jaws. Then the black monster fell over sideways into the water with a thunderous splash, spewing blood and foam into the air.

Jason stared dumbfounded at the area where the shark had vanished for a long moment, not believing what he had just seen.

*Bruce?*

He knew it was him. But how? Then a small flashing light caught his eye and he saw the remote sub pass underneath the surface.

"Harry," he realized.

He heard his name being called from inside the sailboat and ran toward the door.

Beneath the surface, Bruce shook his head from side to side as his murdering teeth sawed Susan to pieces. The shark then opened his mouth and allowed the mutilated body to fall away to the bottom.

"You're not going to let Bruce eat them?" Sarah asked.

"Hell, no!" said Harry. "What if Admiral Zanuck wants to check the shark's stomach? Can you imagine how much trouble we'd be in if they found people inside Bruce's gut?"

Sarah kissed him on the cheek. "That's why I love you."

Jason ran into his friend Ben as he opened the sailboat's door. "Are you alright?" Jason asked.

"I am," said Ben. "But I think Tina's leg is broken. We need to get the inflatable raft out."

Jason shook his head. "No, it's too dangerous for that."

"What is that suppose to mean? Where's Susan?"

"I'll explain later but we're much safer on the boat-"

The sailboat was suddenly hit hard again, this time from the side. Jason and Ben were thrown into the sailboat's living room area, where Tina screamed in agony as she too was thrown across the room.

As the *Amity* was pulled over onto its starboard side Ben crawled over to his injured girlfriend, trying to comfort her as she sobbed.

Jason looked up and saw the room where Ben said that he kept an emergency radio, along with the inflatable raft. He quickly jumped up and ran for it.


Outside, Bruce nearly had the *Amity's* entire bow in his mouth. He sank his teeth into the fiberglass hull as he pulled down, causing the outmatched ship to roll over until it was upside down in the water. Then he pulled down harder until the sailboat was completely submerged.

Now ordered to let go of the sinking boat, Bruce circled the area for a moment. Satisfied that everyone on board was now dead, Harry directed the giant shark back toward his sailboat.

Harry typed in a final command and said, "It's done." He turned in his chair to face Sarah, who rewarded his accomplishment with a kiss on the lips.

"Good job, sailor. Now we're all set."

Several moments after Bruce had disappeared the area where the *Amity* had been pulled under had once again become as calm as a pond. There was no evidence that a horrific murder had taken place there, no blood in the water, no floating debris, no bodies. Just a peaceful current and fireworks in the distance.

Then an orange inflated liferaft shot out from underwater and landed upright on the surface. Jason gasped for air as he held onto the inflatable boat for dear life.

He was very fortunate to be alive. He was too exhausted to move and on the verge of shock. As the fireworks of Oahu lit up the sky in the distance, Jason laid down at the bottom of the liferaft taking deep breaths.

Slowly, exhaustion took a hold of him and he drifted off to sleep.

# 6

Naturally, the media found out about the event.

Because the area where the *Amity* had sunk was more than three-thousand feet deep, the navy had to send manned submersibles down to investigate the wreck. Eventually they announced that the cause of the sinking and the deaths of the four people on board was the result of an attack by orcas and that Jason and his friends had drowned when they became trapped inside their own vessel.

When the news reported the death of Jason Shaw, Sarah had gone to her parents' house pretending to grieve the loss of her brother. At the memorial service she had even given a speech about her loving, caring sibling while pretending to hold back her tears. She had however been told by naval officers to leave out the details of his work for the navy.

Three nights after the incident, on the *Garage Sale*, Harry Jacobs stood pacing on the facality's walkpath with his cell phone to his ear. Sarah stood with her arms folded watching him.

PATRICK D. GALLAHER

"Yes, Admiral Zanuck. No, sir, they haven't. Sir, are you sure that I'm quallified to... Thank you, Admiral. I am truly honored. I will. Thank you, sir." Harry closed his cell phone and stuck it into his pocket. He turned to Sarah. "Guess what? Yours Truly is officially in charge of Project Sea Rex."

Sarah gave him a big white-toothed smile as she walked over and hugged his neck. "Then we're both set for life," she said, kissing him.

"I think this calls for a celebration," said Harry.

Sarah leaned back slightly as she kept her arms around his neck. "I agree. So how about we go below and "celebrate" in private?"

Harry looked down as he felt Sarah move her frontal waist area back and forth across his pants zipper. He looked back into her eyes and saw that she was serious. "See you downstairs."

Sarah kissed him once more and smiled. "I'll be there in a minute."

"Don't keep me waiting."

Sarah waited until he had gone inside and looked for a moment out at the six-foot black dorsal fin cutting through the water in the cage. "Thank you, Bruce," she said. "You have done a great service for us."

35

She turned away to walk toward the door, then stopped. Looking out at sea, she couldn't help but think about her brother. Thanks to his death her father had now given Jason's larger share of his fortune to her. She could now live the rest of her life in absolute luxury.

But was it worth it? Was it really worth murdering her own flesh and blood? Lying to her parents? Did he really deserve to die in such a horrible way?

These and many other questions went through her mind as she stood staring out into the open ocean. After a moment, she finally put her feelings of guilt aside and walked toward the door.

# 7

Jason took off his damp T-shirt and pulled it over his head, doing his best to shield himself from the intense glare of the sun. He laid curled up in the bottom of the inflatable raft throughout his entire first day at sea as a castaway, holding his drying shirt over him in a vain attempt to avoid sunburn.

Bruce had pulled down the *Amity* so fast the night before that he did not have enough time to gather any water or food.

The current had carried him farther out to sea during the night and there was no sign of a ship anywhere on the horizon.

Throughout the afternoon, as his exposed legs took the brunt of the sun's burning rays, the horrific scene of Susan being crushed to death in Bruce's teeth played over and over in his mind. Running into the interior of the sailboat, finding Ben's girlfriend injured and scared.

The sailboat suddenly turning completely upside down, throwing them onto the upturned ceiling and causing Ben's girlfriend to scream in agony. The windows and door exploding as water poured inside. He saw Ben throw himself over his injured girlfriend as a wall of sea water came in through the door, filling the sailboat's interior before Jason could even pull the emergency inflation cord on the inflatable life raft.

Jason had felt panic as his lungs ached for air in the total blackness as the *Amity* was dragged downward. Somehow he had managed to find his way out the broken door and into open water. He then pulled the cord, the inflatable raft instantly expanded and Jason held on for dear life as it shot to the surface.

The terrifying scene played repeatedly in his head throughout the day as Jason would doze off in the bottom of the raft, only to be awakened by the nightmare from the night before. The combined sun burn and horrific memory that would not stop playing in his mind was the worst torture that Jason had ever endured.

Every time he woke up from Bruce's attack he would at first feel frightened, then anger would take over as he remembered who was behind the shark attack.

Harry.

What logical reason could his partner possibly have had to use their own invention to kill him? Sure Jason had given him a hard time, but had he really pushed him to the boiling point? Then he realized the real mastermind behind his murder.

Sarah.

Their father had recently made an excellent living as an oil contractor and had promised in his will that both of his children would each inherit large sums of his fortune. For some reason, Jason was promised a slightly larger share than Sarah.

And with her brother dead she would now take all of his cut. By romancing Harry she could persuade him into using Bruce to attack and kill him under the cover of darkness.

That's why she had asked him where he was going to be for the Fourth of July; she wanted to know where he could be located so that they could ambush him.

Any love that he had previously felt for his sister was quickly replaced with anger. Jason swore that if we were rescued that he would report right away to Admiral Zanuck and have Harry and Sarah put on trial for what they had done. *If* he were ever rescued.

Because of his navy training, Jason knew that having no drinking water on the open ocean meant that he would suffer from dehydration, he would grow weaker and weaker and would eventually waste away until he died, or was rescued.

But Jason knew that the odds of a small raft being found in the middle of the vast ocean, especially the Pacific, was very slim. He began to wish that Bruce had eaten him rather than to go through a slow death like this.

Not counting on a rescue ship anytime soon, Jason began to accept the fact that his fate was sealed and that the sun would burn him to a dry corpse for the sea gulls to feast on.

And so one uncomfortable, dry-mouthed, sunburned day began to blend into the next in an unending routine.

# 8

The sea was quiet and a gentle breeze could be felt as the orange raft floated on the flat ocean surface for the fifth day since the sinking of the *Amity*.

Jason could not feel the breeze as he sat motionless in the raft. He was sitting upright and had laid his shirt over his face. His skin was beginning to turn dangerously red and it hurt for him to move. He was very thirsty and his mouth and tongue were completely dry.

He just wished that the sun would kill him already, that another shark would jump into the raft and pull him down. Anything would be better than this unbareable heat.

His vision was becoming foggy and he dosed off repeatedly as he sat perfectly still in the raft that was now beginning to deflate. Soon it would lose all of its air and begin to sink from underneath him, and he would be too weak to swim.

Jason dozed off again and failed to notice the ship that came up alongside, its masts full of sails blocking out the sun. The name on the bow that came into focus read: *CHRISSIE*.

Jason stirred partially as he felt something jump into the raft with him. His eyes suddenly fluttered open then tinsed as someone pulled the shirt off of his head. A woman's face suddenly came into focus as she moved in front of him.

She was very beautiful. Her long red hair framed a soft face with full lips. A pair of deep blue eyes examined Jason as she checked his pulse.

"He's alive!" she shouted in a Russian accent. The woman took out a bottle of water and brought it up to his mouth.

Jason gulped down the cold liquid very fast. He tried to say something but couldn't. His mouth was still too dry. His vision blurred and he began to drift into unconciousness once more.

He heard the woman say, "Don't worry, sir. We're going to help you."

Then everything went black.

# 9

He stepped out onto the deck wondering how he got there.

Jason couldn't believe it. How was it possible? He was standing on the deck of the **Amity**. The moon was full and it cast its light down on the endless ocean that surrounded the sailboat.

Jason suddenly felt joy like he hadn't felt in days. If the **Amity** was still here, then his friends must still be alive as well. He ran inside, expecting to find Ben, Susan and Tina waiting for him. But the room was empty.

He was drawn back out onto the deck by the sound of something splashing in the water. Jason didn't want to go to the boat's edge. He knew what was waiting for him there but he felt drawn to the sound of whatever was in the water.

A black six-foot dorsal fin cut across the glass-like surface as it sped toward the **Amity** off the port side.

Bruce.

Jason watched hypnotized as the fin disappeared just before reaching the boat. He felt his heart racing as he stared into the black water below him, but he couldn't move. Then the ocean exploded and the giant shark's murderous jaws came up toward him.

Jason jolted upright in bed with the sensation of being shocked with electricity in his brain. It was just a dream, he realized. Just a dream.

*Wait a minute. How did I get into a bed? Where's the raft?*

Jason realized that he had been rehydrated when he felt his mouth and tongue wet. The clothes that he had been wearing when he was castawayed on the raft had been removed and he was now wearing a navy blue T-shirt and what appeared to be swim shorts. He looked around the room that he was in. A beam of sunlight streaming in through a small round window revealed that he was in some kind of ship cabin.

Jason suddenly felt like he was in a scene from 20,000 Leagues Under the Sea, waking up on Captain Nemo's submarine after being shipwrecked. He threw the blanket off of him, walked to the door and opened it. He was surprised that it was not locked.

He stepped out into a short hall and followed the sound of voices as he walked up a short flight of stairs that led up to the deck. As he came up into the sunlight, Jason found the crew that had rescued him hard at work.

The ship that he found himself on was a sleek, three-masted tall ship, at least two-hundred feet long. Its white sails were open and the wind pushed it across the ocean surface. A single funnel stack rose between the first and second masts but Jason assumed that the engine room it led down to was only used when needed.

A rectangle piece of metal dropped from the upper deck and onto the floor in front of him. Jason picked it up. It was a license plate from Louisiana. He looked above him as he heard the familiar Russian accent of the woman that had boarded his raft. She and two men were digging into the cut stomach of a tiger shark that hung by its tail from the mast.

"Dammit Simon!" the woman said. "You know better than littering the deck like that. Are you trying to get yourself thrown overboard?"

"Who died and made you captain?" the man joked.

The woman was clearly frustrated with her partner as she jumped down onto the lower deck in front of Jason. She wore only a white loose-fitting shirt and a blue bikini underneath. Her hands were covered in the dead shark's blood and some of the red fluid had spilled onto the front of her clothing as well. She turned to find Jason standing there looking at her.

She was the most beautiful woman that Jason had ever seen. Her red hair framed a soft face with full lips. Her deep blue eyes widened slightly in surprise as she turned and realized that he was there. Her skin was tanned, evident of a life spent working under the sun. She was about Jason's age, at least in her mid-twenties.

Jason quickly searched his memory, but without success. He was certain that he had never laid eyes on a woman like this before.

"Oh," the woman said. "You're awake."

Jason found himself unable to speak at first. "Yah," he said finally. "I'm sorry. Can you please tell me where I am?"

"You're on board the barque *Chrissie*. In the middle of the Pacific."

"How long have I been out?"

"Three days," the woman answered him. "My name is Natalia. The captain was wanting to speak with you as soon as you felt well enough to do so." She looked at the bloody license plate in his hand. "Why don't you let me have that and I'll take you to her."

*Her?* Jason thought. *The captain is a 'her?'* He handed Natalia the license plate and she tossed it back up to the upper deck.

"Simon. I'm taking our guest to see Maria. And unless you want to be dropped off at the next desert island you had better clean up that mess when you're finished."

Jason couldn't help but watch as Natalia wiped the tiger shark's blood from her hands as they walked to the bridge together. She noticed his stare and gave him a shy smile. Jason had only just met Natalia but he already noticed something about her considerate personality and toughness that he found very appealing.

They walked onto the bridge where an older Spanish woman looked at them over a log book. She was tall and wore a sleeveless shirt and light pants. Her long, dark hair was straight and flowed down her back. She was old enough to be Jason's mother, but the only clue to that fact were a few strands of gray that fell from her forehead.

"Maria," said Natalia. "Our guest has finally awakened." She turned and smiled at Jason as she walked back out of the bridge, leaving him alone with the captain.

Jason turned and watched her leave as Natalia returned to her job of gutting the tiger shark. He turned back to Maria as she began to speak.

"Well. It's good to see you up and about. What is your name?"

Jason was surprised when she politely extended her hand. He shook it. "Shaw," he said. "Doctor Jason Shaw."

"My name is Maria. I'm the captain of the *Chrissie*."

"If I may ask, Captain. What kind of ship am I on exactly?"

"We're survivalists, Doctor Shaw. My crew mainly consists of people who are eager to get away from the hardships of their past lives and live on their own terms as free men and women."

Jason suddenly felt a little concerned about what Maria was saying. It sounded as if she was giving a justified speech for living a care-free life as an ocean-going thief. Now he was hoping that he had not fallen into the wrong company.

"You're not pirates, are you?" he asked carefully.

Maria did not appear at all flattered by his question as her smile turned into a frown. "I said that we were survivalists. I didn't say that we were criminals."

Jason felt alarmed as Maria walked up to him and put her hand on his shoulder.

"Doctor Shaw, I was once a hard-working woman in my native country of Spain. After I became divorced nothing could seem to go right for me. I was always struggling to make ends meet, working to keep a roof over my head, and slaving myself by any means necessary to make the politicians back home richer. Then one day they came and threatened to take my home because of overdue taxes. It was then that I decided that enough was enough and I sought to escape from it all.

"Fortunately, I have always had a love for the sea. So I spent all of my remaining money on this ship, burned down my house and set sail for the open ocean. Ask any member of my crew and they will tell you a similiar story about their own lives.

"No, Doctor Shaw. We are not pirates. We are not outlaws. We are free men and women who have a love for adventure. The crew of the *Chrissie* live off of the sea and dry land, not off of criminal acts. I had nearly everything taken from me and I would never forgive myself for stealing from someone else."

Jason was intrigued by Maria's story. He had never quite met a person like her before. The story that she was telling him, about living life to the fullest free from the debts of society, was a completely foreign concept to him. He felt that if he were to talk to her long enough that she might be able to persuade him into the same lifestyle.

"Now it's your turn, Doctor Shaw," said Maria. "What is your story? How did you end up on a rubber raft in the middle of nowhere?"

Jason hesitated to say anything at first. "You wouldn't believe me if I told you."

Maria sat down in her captain's seat. "Try me."

Jason then proceeded to explain to Maria the details of his recent ordeal. He told her all about Project Sea Rex, about Bruce, about the attack on the *Amity* and his partner and sister's betrayal.

Jason realized at one point in the conversation that he didn't need to be concerned about telling her everything about the top secret project that he had been assigned to. Maria had cut herself off from the rest of society so there would be no concern of her giving these secrets away to another country.

Once he had finished Maria found herself unable to respond for a moment as if she were astounded by his tale. "That is an interesting story Doctor Shaw," she said finally. "What do you plan to do when you return home?"

"Expose Sarah and Jacobs for their crime obviously."

"How do you plan to do it?"

Jason shook his head. "I'm still working on that."

"Well you will have plenty of time to think about it," said Maria. "We won't be stopping near Hawaii for a while. But you are welcomed to join me and my crew for the time being."

Jason looked out the window of the bridge as he considered her offer. There was no telling how long it would be before he would be able to contact Admiral Zanuck and have Harry and Sarah brought to justice. But then again what choice did he have? For the moment, the *Chrissie* was his only hope of ever getting back home someday.

He also noticed Natalia working on the upper deck with the other crew members. The idea of sailing across the ocean with her made him feel like it would be worth the wait.

After a moment Jason finally turned back to Maria. "Alright, Captain. I accept. For now, consider me a member of your crew."

# 10

At first Maria had allowed Jason to remain on board the *Chrissie* as a guest. She had informed him that they would return him to Hawaii whenever their voyage had required them to stop there for supplies. As time went by, however, Jason insisted on helping the others out with their duties. Soon he became a full time and respected member of Maria's crew.

During one stop at a desert island Jason had noticed one of the other crew members, a trouble-making braggart named Robert, talking to Natalia. She was clearly annoyed by his obvious attempt to romance her into his cabin that night as she stared at him with her arms folded.

Jason finally decided to intervene and came up behind Robert as he carried a basket of fruit. "Natalia. Could you look at some of this fruit for me please?"

Robert turned his head to look back over his shoulder at him. "Get lost, new guy. Can't you see that I'm talking to her?"

"Anyone can see that she doesn't want to talk to you, pal."

Robert turned around to face him, accepting Jason's insult as a challenge to a fight. Jason stood firm as he placed the basket on the ground, ready to take him on. But before Robert could take two steps Maria called out from down the beach.

"Robert. If you don't want to stay on this island you had better get back to work. Now."

Robert looked at Jason once more and then walked away.

Natalia approached Jason and said, "Thank you."

Jason nodded. "My pleasure."

They looked at each other for a moment, each one wanting to say something more, then returned to their duties.

Later that day, as they were preparing to cast off, Jason found himself alone on the bridge with Maria. He eyed Natalia as she walked into the cargo bay with a jug of water.

"Captain," he said. "Tell me about Natalia."

Maria looked over at the young Russian woman and then back at Jason. "She's a mysterious one. I found her about three years ago off the Mexican coast. We had stumbled upon what appeared to be an abandoned research ship. When we boarded to investigate I found her handcuffed below decks, starving and frightened out of her mind. She still won't tell me where she came from, but whatever happened to her was not good."

Jason's eyed opened wide as he woke up from another nightmare of a shark attack. He laid in bed for a moment, taking deep breaths as the electric shocks in his brain subsided. It occurred to him that these repeated nightmares might prevent him from ever getting a full night's sleep again.

He slowly sat up in his bed and rubbed his eyes. Feeling the need for fresh air he left his cabin and walked out onto the *Chrissie's* deck.

It was still dark outside and the night sky was filled with hundreds of stars. He placed his hands on the ship's wooden rail as he breathed in the salt air and listened to the sound of the ocean in the darkness.

It had been five months since he had cheated death after his fatal encounter with Bruce and had become a member of Maria's crew. He had spent every day since his rescue plotting his revenge against Harry and Sarah, thinking of numerous ways to expose them for their crime. Now he finally had a plan that seemed flawless. All that was needed was to get back to Hawaii and contact Admiral Zanuck.

But during the voyage there had also appeared another piece of the plan that he had not expected, and he wasn't sure about what to do about it yet.

It was Natalia.

Over the past five months the two of them had become more friendly and often engaged in cheerful conversations. Natalia was a strong woman who could hold her own, and yet as he came to know her more Jason could also sense a softness about her that he found irresistable. She was also very private, not wishing to reveal too much about herself.

Maria, however, had come to notice how cheerful and more open Natalia had become toward Jason since they had first met.

Before long, Jason realized that he had fallen for her. But he also knew very little about her. He remembered what Maria had said about finding her chained inside of a deserted yacht and wasn't sure how to get her to tell him about her secret past. If he was going to reveal his love to her he first needed to know more about her.

"You can't sleep either?"

Jason looked to his right to find Natalia walking toward him. She was wearing only a long shirt that covered her like a small dress but exposed her long slender legs.

"Not without getting eaten by my pet shark," said Jason.

"Would you like some company? Unless you would prefer to be alone-"

"No, it's okay," Jason assured her. "I could actually use some good company."

Natalia smiled. "Good. Me, too." She stood next to him gazing up at the star-filled sky for a while. "Aren't they lovely?"

"What?" Jason asked.

"The stars. They're so pretty tonight."

"Really? I wasn't looking at the stars."

Natalia realized that Jason was staring at her. She gave him a girlish smile as she brushed some strands of red hair blowing in front of her face behind her ear. "So have you figured out how you're going to get your revenge yet?"

Jason nodded. "I believe that I've got it all figured out."

"What is your plan?"

"I'm going to keep the details to myself for now, but let's just say that they won't see me coming."

Natalia nodded. "Well I wish you the best of luck then."

Jason then remembered what Maria had told him about Natalia earlier that afternoon. Without anymore hesitation he decided to go ahead and ask her. "Natalia, could I ask you a question? You don't have to answer it if you don't want to."

"What is it?" she asked.

"What happened to you? How did you end up handcuffed in an abandoned ship in the middle of the ocean?"

Natalia looked down into the sea as she considered his question. For a moment, Jason didn't think that she was going to say anything.

"My mother had died giving birth to me so the only real family that I had ever known was my father. He was a treasure hunter. One day he took me on one of his voyages to the Mexican coast. We were looking for buried treasure from nineteenth century Mexico."

"I've heard of this treasure before," said Jason. "During the Mexican War of the 1840s, Santa Anna sent a small ship loaded with treasure out into the Pacific to keep it from falling into the hands of the invading American Army. But the ship disappeared outside of the Sea of Cortez."

Natalia smiled. "That is correct. Anyway, after years of research my father was convinced that he had discovered the treasure's exact location on the island of Isla de Guadalupe and wanted to find it himself. He told me to come along with him, and I did. I thought that for once he wanted to spend some social time with me, and have an adventure with his daughter.

"We found the treasure exactly where he said it would be. But then something unexpected happened. We were joined by another Russian ship, whose captain told my father that he needed to load the gold on board his vessel and erase all evidence of our being there by scuttling our yacht. When I asked him what was going on my father informed me that the Russian Secret Service had sent him to find and steal the treasure out from under the Mexican Government's nose.

"After the scuttling charge was placed and the treasure was loaded onto the other ship, one of the other Russian sailors grabbed me, took me downstairs and handcuffed me to a metal pipe. As it turned out, they were to eliminate all the witnesses to their little treasure theft and I was to die when the ship pulled me down to the bottom. My father didn't even try to stop them. When it came down to it all, he was more loyal to his government than he was to his own daughter. He never even came down to tell me that he was sorry, or to say good bye.

"But when the other vessel pulled away and they activated the scuttling charge it was their ship that exploded. I had sensed that my father would betray me somehow, so instead of placing the explosive scuttling charge on the keel of our yacht as ordered, I hid it underneath the powder magazine of theirs.

"After that, I sat there with my hands cuffed above my head waiting for someone to come and help me. Three days passed before I heard human voices again, heard the sound of footsteps on deck, and then Maria came into the room and rescued me. I have been with her crew ever since."

Jason found himself unable to respond as he listened intently to her story. He stared at her throughout the entire tale and suddenly found a new respect for the young Russian woman that had rescued him five months earlier.

Natalia looked out over the ocean as she wrapped up her story. "It is the worst feeling in the world to be betrayed by your own flesh and blood."

"I know what that's like," said Jason. "When I realized that my one and only sister was behind my attempted murder, and I saw everything that I held dear taken away from me, I was so heart broken. I just wanted to curl up in the bottom of that life raft and die because I felt like I had no reason to live anymore. And then I found you."

Natalia suddenly turned to face him, surprised by his confession of his feelings for her. She opened her mouth to say something in response but could not find the words.

Jason suddenly realized that Natalia had been waiting for him to say something to her for a while. He kept his eyes focused on hers as he reached out and gently took both of her hands into his. "I love you, Natalia. I have been looking for you throughout my entire life and I don't want to live another day without you."

Natalia smiled, then moved forward and they both put their arms around each other at the same time. Jason encompassed his arms around Natalia as he held her tight, finding comfort in her embrace while she did the same in his. He could not remember a time when he had felt so good in his heart as he held her in close.

Jason found it hard to let go of her as they both stood underneath the starlit sky. He was convinced that this was who he had been looking for his entire life, who he was destined to be with forever. Jason felt such relief in that moment as he embraced his soulmate.

Natalia may not have been part of his original plans, but she certainly was now.

# 11

*Jason swam up toward the moonlight, his lungs bursting for air as his head broke the surface.*

*He was scared.*

*He knew that the great fish was close but he couldn't see it. He looked around frantically, trying to find it before it came for him. The more he searched for it, the more scared he became. How did he get there? What was he doing in the water? Where is the shark?*

*He turned around just in time to see the black dorsal fin cut through the water toward him and disappear. Then the giant shark exploded out of the ocean and came down on top of him, jaws agape...*

"Jason?"

Jason opened his eyes wide as he woke up from the terrifying nightmare. For a brief instant he laid flat on his back then cried out in terror as he quickly sat up and grabbed onto flesh.

He suddenly realized that he was looking up at Natalia as she knelt next to him, his hands squeezing the biceps of her arms. He took deep breaths and let go of her as he relaxed. He was lying inside of a sleeping bag that was laid out on the rugged ground that he rested on.

Jason, Natalia and a few other crew members of the *Chrissie* were spending the night on Isla de Guadalupe, an almost barren island that consisted of two ancient overlapping volcanoes, the highest of which was situated to the north. Located about 150 miles off the coast of Baja California, it's only twenty-two miles long north and south and 5.9 miles wide east and west. At the most, only twenty people actually inhabit the volcanic island.

Maria had permitted her crew to spend the night there in order to get some shore leave. Most of Isla de Guadalupe's coast consists of rocky bluffs so the crew had to stay on the island's southern end where the shore angles down into the water.

The moon was full and shone bright. Jason guessed that it was sometime after midnight.

"It was only a dream, Darling," said Natalia.

"I'm sorry," Jason exhaled. "I'm sorry if I hurt you."

"You didn't hurt me, but you had me terribly worried. When I came over here you were moving back and forth and even crying in your sleep like you were being tortured to death."

Jason wiped away the tears beneath his eyes. The nightmare had felt so real, the terror of reliving the giant shark's attack haunting him every time he closed his eyes was unbareable.

"The things I would give to have a full night's sleep again."

Natalia put her hands on his neck and hugged his head against her chest as she tried to comfort him.

As Jason put his hands on her back he could feel no clothing, only skin. He gently pushed Natalia away to get a better look. She was dressed in a red bikini that revealed a slim, curved body that would have made a supermodel jealous.

"Are you about to go swimming?" Jason asked.

"Yes," said Natalia. "I was coming to wake you up because I want you to join me."

"I'd love to but why can't it wait until tomorrow?"

"Because I want to show you something and I don't want the others to know about it." She grabbed his hand and pulled him to his feet. "Come on."

Natalia began running down toward the island's shore, smiling and looking over her shoulder to make sure that Jason was following her. As soon as the first wave lapped against her ankles she dove in and began stroking out into the open ocean.

Jason pursued the red-haired beauty all the way to the water's edge, then stopped. He hesitated as he watched the waves crash against the rocky shore, unable to move any further.

Natalia turned onto her back as she stroked farther out, lifting a tanned leg skyward and then sinking backwards beneath the waves. When she resurfaced, she realized that Jason was still on the shore. "Come into the water," she called out.

Her smile faded as she realized that something was wrong. She swam back to the shore and walked onto the sloping rock dripping wet, where Jason stood as nervous as someone about to perform his first skydive.

"Natalia," Jason said. "I'm sorry, but I can't do it. I just... I can't believe this. I work for the navy, I shouldn't be afraid of the water."

"Is it because of the shark?"

Jason nodded, embaressed.

"Jason," Natalia assured him. "If what you say is true then Bruce is locked up thousands of miles away in Hawaii. He is not here." She took his hand in hers. "I am here."

Jason gently squeezed her hand as Natalia restored his courage.

"Come with me." Natalia held his hand tight as she led him into the water. They walked until the waves were up to their chests then stroked to a deep area farther out.

PATRICK D. GALLAHER

About a hundred yards from the shore, Natalia grabbed onto Jason's hand once more. "We're here," she said. "Are you ready?"

Jason nodded, then they both took a deep breath and dove.

# 12

As Jason and Natalia swam straight down, the outline of a ship's broken hull resting on the ocean floor came into view, perfectly illuminated by the moonlight. The vessel was broken into two parts as if it had been blown open from the inside out by a powerful explosion. The bow and stern were separated by only a few feet, sitting perfectly upright and facing each other as if the two severed halfs of the ship wished to be welded back together once more.

Jason recognized the vessel as he swam closer to it, which appeared to be a fishing trawler. It was a Russian *Stalingrad*-class ship. Although techincally classified as naval yachts, these were actually spy ships of the Russian Navy that mostly patrolled areas of the Western Pacific. But this ship was resting on the bottom only a hundred miles off the Mexican coast.

What is it doing here? Jason wondered.

Then he remembered the story that Natalia had told him. As they descended upon the wreck Jason looked at her in disbelief, wondering if this was her father's pirate vessel that she had blown up three years before. As if reading his mind she looked at him and nodded.

Natalia then pointed toward the spy ship's severed front section. She swam over the bridge toward the bow and down onto the deck. Jason swam up alongside her as Natalia stopped at a closed hatch and motioned for him to join her. He found a rusted crowbar and with both of their strengths they managed to pry the hatch up.

Natalia immediatly swam down into the now open hatchway and disappeared in the pitch black room below. Jason followed as fast as he could, his lungs were now beginning to ache for air and he knew that Natalia was eager to get back to the surface as well.

He descended into a dark room, the white beam of the moon's glow coming in from the hatchway their only source of light. He felt a hand grab his shoulder and Natalia gestured for him to help her lift a rectangle metal crate off the floor. It had Russian lettering on it that he couldn't read. As he lifted it, Jason could feel that it was heavy and wondered what was inside it.

Before they swam back up and out the hatchway he looked around, and realized that there were at least several dozen more identical crates lying scattered across the ship's floor.

A few minutes later, Jason and Natalia emerged back onto the rocky shore carrying the metal crate between them as they took it inland. They finally knelt down and Jason used the crowbar that he had retrieved from the wreck to peal it open like a sardine can. As they opened it and turned it over, sea water spilled out. And so did a small waterfall of Spanish gold coins, pearl necklaces, diamond rings and rubies.

Jason fell to his knees. He found himself unable to speak as he stared in awe at the treasure that now lay before him.

"What do you think?" Natalia asked, kneeling next to him.

Jason gathered some of the treasure up in his hands. "Is this what's in all of those crates down there?"

Natalia nodded. "My father really hit the jackpot. He was suppose to take all of this back to Russia where it would then be secretly cashed in as financial gain for the Motherland."

"Natalia, why are you showing this to me?"

"I thought that perhaps it would be good for us to have once we returned to civilization again."

"We?"

Natalia nodded. "I would like to go with you when you return to Hawaii, if you will have me."

Jason was unable to answer at first. He had been wanting to ask Natalia to come back with him for some time but was not certain if she would agree to. Now that one question was out of the way there was only one other thing he needed to ask her.

He looked back down at the spilled treasure and picked up a golden ring encrusted with a clear diamond. He held up the ring for her to see.

"Natalia," he said. "Nothing in the world would make me happier than for you to join me for the rest of my life."

He took her left hand and slid the ring onto her finger as Natalia put her right hand over her mouth. She then embraced him as she began to cry.

"I love you, Natalia Ravoc," said Jason.

"I love you, Jason Shaw," said Natalia.

After a moment, they finally let go of each other and Jason wiped the tears falling from her eyes.

"So what will we buy with all of this treasure?" Natalia asked.

"I have two immediate things in mind," said Jason. "First. A private wedding ceremony for us in Hawaii."

"And the second?"

Jason looked out to the northwest as his mind returned to the people who had tried to kill him.

"Revenge."

# 13

Finally, after ten months of sailing across the Pacific Ocean, Jason Shaw was finally returning home.

The *Chrissie* was at last coming within sight of the Hawaiian Islands. The tall ship sailed up to the island of Maui, staying a safe distance from the shore as Jason and Natalia prepared to depart for the final time toward the beach. After gathering what little personal belongings that they pocessed into a boat, Maria stood talking to them as they said their good byes.

"You two take care of each other. No matter what happens, no matter how far away we are, both of you will always hold a special place among my crew."

"Thank you for everything, Maria," said Jason.

Natalia said nothing as she embraced her captain of three years for the final time. Jason embraced her as well before Maria tearfully stepped back and watched them drive away in their boat back to the beach.

Natalia sat smiling next to Jason in the wooden motorboat as they headed off to start a new life together, with the metal crate of treasure sitting at the bottom of the boat beneath their feet.

Jason and Natalia stood holding hands on the beach of Lahaina for almost an hour watching as the sailing ship that had been Jason's home for almost a year, and Natalia's home for three years, sailed away into the horizon until it could be seen no more.

Jason then turned to his fiancee. They both had a lot to do now that they were back home, and not much time to do it.

Jason had chosen to be dropped off on Maui instead of Oahu because Lahaina Beach was one of the most romantic locations in the Hawaiian Islands. The perfect place to exchange vows.

That evening, just prior to sunset, Jason hired a priest to have him and Natalia married in a private ceremony. Natalia looked stunning as she stood in front of Jason that evening. She was wearing a pure white dress that came down to her feet and a ring of colored flowers crowned her head as they held each other's hands.

The ceremony was short and as it concluded Jason cupped his wife's soft face in his hands and gently kissed her sweet lips.

One week later, they had secretly purchased themselves a sailing yacht and were on their way back to Oahu to see Admiral Zanuck.

# 14

Jason wasn't sure what he would say as he and Natalia were driven by taxi to the house of Admiral Carl Zanuck outside of Honolulu. His biggest concern was that he would give his former boss a heart attack as he thought that he was looking at a ghost.

He could feel Natalia gently squeezing his hand and he turned and smiled at her. From the moment they had become husband and wife one week before Jason had found it hard to let go of Natalia. She was a rare woman. Over the past year she had helped him heal from the wounds-both physical and psycholgical-that the shark had inflicted upon him. Both of them had even come to notice how Jason's night terrors of shark attacks had stopped haunting his dreams ever since they began going to sleep together.

Jason knew that he would need her support in the coming weeks if he was going to bring his friends' murderers to justice. He had told her his plans to get his payback against Harry and Sarah and had asked for her to help him. To his amazement, she agreed and even insisted on meeting Admiral Zanuck in person.

After a long drive, the Admiral's home came into view, complete with an iron fence and a guard at the gate.

"Is this the place?" the taxi driver asked.

"Yes it is," answered Jason.

The guard stood at the gate of the Admiral's home, hand firmly on his pistol as he watched the couple pay the taxi driver and turn to meet him. "Can I help you with something, sir?"

Jason couldn't believe that this man was still here after ten months. He had never gotten to know Lieutenant Michael Gary personally in his past visits to Admiral Zanuck's house, but he had remembered his name and Gary had come to recognize Jason enough to the point where he wouldn't have bothered to ask for his ID. But now it had been almost a year since his last visit and the guard had obviously forgotten him.

"Don't you recognize me, Michael?" Jason asked.

The guard looked confused. "Do I know you, sir?"

"You should. I used to visit Admiral Zanuck quite often."

"Do you have any ID, sir?"

Jason shook his head. "I'm afraid not."

"What's your name, sir?"

"Jason Shaw."

The name left Lieutenant Gary speechless, and stunned.

Admiral Zanuck raced home in his car upon hearing the news.

He had been in the middle of a meeting with other officers under his command when he was told that he had an emergency call from home. His wife had told him about Jason's return from the dead and said that he wanted to see the Admiral as soon as possible. After hanging up the phone Zanuck immediatly cancelled the meeting, got into his car and began quickly driving home as fast as he could.

Lieutenant Gary opened the gate for him as the Admiral raced through. Zanuck quickly parked the car and walked in.

"Where is he?" he asked his wife.

Miss Zanuck pointed into the living room where Jason and Natalia sat holding hands on the couch. They both stood as Admiral Zanuck slowly approached them, eyes widened in disbelief.

"Hello, sir," said Jason.

Zanuck said nothing as he put his hands on Jason's shoulders and looked him over, making sure that it was really him. "Where in the hell have you been all this time, boy?"

Jason sighed. "It's a long and ugly story, Admiral."

Zanuck eyed Natalia, who nervously rubbed the wedding ring on her finger, then looked at Jason again.

"I want to hear it! All of it!"

For the next hour Jason filled the Admiral in on his story, starting with Bruce's attack on the *Amity*, Harry Jacobs' betrayel, being castawayed on the open ocean, his rescue and adventures across the Pacific, and his recent marriage to Natalia.

Zanuck massaged his forehead as he came to realize the truth. He stood up and began pacing the room as Jason finished his story. "Are you certain that it was your shark?" he asked.

"I'm positive, sir," said Jason. "I even saw the remote mini-sub that we designed to guide Bruce underwater."

Zanuck turned his back to the sitting couple. Jason could tell that he was furious and wondered if he was going to start throwing things across the room. "Gaah!" the Admiral cried out. "I'm gonna ring Jacobs' neck for this. Did you know I gave that bastard your job as head of Project Sea Rex? He'll be on his knees begging for mercy when I'm threw with him."

"Actually, Admiral," said Jason, "I was going to ask that you wait a little while before doing that."

"Why?"

"Because I believe that someone else was involved in it with him."

"Who?"

"My sister, Sarah. I'd bet my bottom dollar that she sweet-talked him into killing me so that she could get my share of our father's inheritance."

"That would make sense," said Zanuck. "The two of them have been living like royalty since your death, buying brand new expensive cars and jewelry, going on vacations in different countries."

"How are my parents by the way?"

"They're fine. They moved back to California shortly after your disappearence. Your mother was absolutely devastated at your funeral, which was beautiful by the way."

Jason smiled at the Admiral's joke.

Zanuck hesitated before continuing. "Your sister even gave a heart-warming speech about you."

"She's always been a talented liar," said Jason.

"If what you say is true," said Zanuck, "if she is involved in your attempted murder, you're gonna need proof in order to convict her as well."

"That's why I'm here, Admiral. I've been thinking about how to get both of them for almost a year and I finally have a plan, but I'll need your help."

Zanuck sat back down as Jason caught his attention.

"Tell me what you need."

# 15

The USS *Missouri* was an Iowa-class battleship with a proud history that extended all the way back to World War II. She had taken part in numerous battles that included Iwo Jima and Okinawa, the Japanese Instrument of Surrender that offically ended the war was signed on her deck and she even survived an Iraqi missile attack during the First Gulf War in 1991.

But since 1999 this battle hardened veteran had served as a museum ship for numerous visitors. She now sat docked at Ford Island, her bow pointed north toward the white memorial that straddled the sunken hull of the battleship *Arizona*, sunk during the Japanese attack on Pearl Harbor in 1941. While the *Arizona* memorial symbolized the beginning of the Second World War, the *Missouri* represented its end.

The forward deck of the "Mighty Mo" as she was sometimes called was filled with naval officers from different countries. They were from Japan, Great Britain, Australia, India, and of course the United States. Flags from each of the nations present for the yearly RIMPAC naval exercises fluttered in the morning breeze as Admiral Zanuck stood at the podium in his crisp white uniform, welcoming each country as he gave a speech before the nations' fleets sailed out into the open ocean the next day.

Standing amidst the civilian audience that included the families and other guests was a couple that anyone would have taken for a pair of rich foreign tourists. Jason was dressed in a blue and white Aloha shirt and white shorts. His face had become more tanned since his voyage across the Pacific. A fake beard had been applied to his lower jaw and a pair of contact lenses had turned his eyes from brown to blue.

Jason smiled with the arrogance of a man who had too much money in his pocket, which was exactly the kind of attitude that Admiral Zanuck had advised him to act out for this to work.

Natalia, holding onto his arm as they watched Admiral Zanuck's speech, was wearing a blue dress that exposed her entire left shoulder. A wide-brimmed hat shielded her face from the hot sun.

Both of them also wore thick sunglasses and rings of flowers that hung from their necks.

Out of the corner of her eye Natalia noticed another couple walk past her as they looked for a place to stand among the crowd. Both of them were shorter than Jason and Natalia, the man standing at about five feet, nine inches. The woman was blonde-haired and her companion wore wire-rimmed glasses.

Jason couldn't help but grin at himself as he watched Harry Jacobs and his sister Sarah walk past him out of the corner of his eye.

Harry had shaved his scraggly beard and had straightened his curly hair since his attempt to kill Jason nearly a year before.

Sarah, however, had not changed at all. She had obviously put the money that had been meant for her older sibling toward her own personal satisfaction. She wore a striking red dress that exposed her entire back and expensive jewelry decorated her fingers, neck, ears, and a piercing was also visible on her nose. They found a place among the other civilians and stood listening to the Admiral's speech.

"Is that them?" asked Natalia, her voice enough to where only her husband could hear her.

Jason nodded. "That's them."

"Your sister seems to be more self-absorbed than I expected."

Jason grinned. "That's an understatement. Wait until you meet her."

After the ceremony had been concluded, the naval officers and civilian guests stood around talking and enjoying the snack table.

Admiral Zanuck stood and smiled as he greeted guests and other foreign naval officers.

"Admiral." Harry Jacobs and Sarah Shaw walked up to Zanuck and shook his hand.

"Harry. Miss Shaw. Thank you for coming." Zanuck was doing his best to maintain his smile as he confronted the two people that he now realized had been lying to him about Jason's death for almost a year.

"Admiral Zanuck," came a Russian voice. Jason and Natalia walked arm in arm up to him.

"Mister Ravoc," said Zanuck. "Doctor Jacobs. Miss Shaw. Allow me to introduce Joseph and Natalia Ravoc. They are our special guests here today."

Both couples smiled and shook hands as they introduced each other.

There was no sign of recognition from Harry or Sarah as they unknowingly looked into the eyes of the man whom they were certain they had killed off nearly a year before. Jason was pleased that his disguise was working flawlessly.

Sarah looked at Natalia with envy as she studied her. Natalia could tell that she was both astounded and jealous of her beauty as she admired her tall, slim figure.

Eventually both the men and women broke away from each other to talk. As Sarah and Natalia engaged in conversation with drinks in hand Natalia asked, "So tell me, Miss Shaw. Do you have family here?"

Sarah sighed. "My parents moved back to California about a year ago because they couldn't bare being here anymore."

"Really? I was told that Hawaii was paradise. What could possibly make them want to leave?"

"About a year ago, my older brother was killed in an accident with some friends off the coast."

"Well, I'm sorry to hear that. How did that happen?"

"An orca capsized their boat."

Natalia put her hand over her heart, trying to act sympathetic. "An orca?"

"It broke my parents' hearts."

"Well, I'll bet it was very hard for you as well."

Sarah quickly looked for a way out of the conversation by trying to change the subject. "Miss Ravoc, I have to say are you are a gorgeous woman. Are you a model?"

Natalia smiled. "Heavens, no. But thank you for the compliment. Actually, my husband and I are adventurers. We purchased our own yacht earlier this year to sail out and see the world."

Sarah then noticed Natalia's golden diamond ring that outshined the two she had on her own hand. "He must make some serious money to be able to buy that for you."

Natalia lifted her hand to show her the Spanish gold ring that shone like the sun. "Oh this old thing?" she said. "This is just one piece of sunken treasure that we found off the coast of Mexico. In fact, we're going back there after this to get the rest of it."

"What?" Sarah asked.

Natalia stood there with her mouth open as she suddenly realized what she had said. "I mean, we've purchased some more jewelry in Mexico and we have to go pick it up."

Sarah noticed Natalia's husband come up behind her and kiss her on the cheek. "Darling," he said. "I think it's time for us to go."

"I think you're right," Natalia agreed. "It was very nice to meet you, Miss Shaw."

Sarah shook her hand. "Likewise, Miss Ravoc. Safe journeys on your next adventure." She then turned to Natalia's husband, not realizing that she was looking into the eyes of her own flesh and blood brother. "Take care, Mister Ravoc."

Jason smiled as he politely shook her hand. "Thank you, Miss Shaw. It was such a delight to meet you as well."

Natalia then took her husband's arm and the two of them walked away into the crowd.

Sarah watched them go. She hardly even noticed Harry come up to her as she stared at the departing Russian couple with interest.

Jason continued to look straight ahead at their exit off the ship as Natalia held onto him in the crowd. "You didn't tell her about our secret treasure, did you?"

Natalia smiled. "Never."

"You didn't tell her where it was, did you?"

"Of course not."

Jason smiled as he gently squeezed her hand. "Good job."

# 16

Two nights later, at the floating assylum known as the *Garage Sale*, Sarah stood with her hands on the metal rail. She looked down from the balcony staring at the giant shark's six-foot black dorsal fin cutting across the surface, lost in thought. Another idea was forming in her head as she watched Harry's giant pet, Bruce, endlessly circle its cage like a pacing tiger. She was so focused on the evil scheme forming in her head that she didn't notice Harry walk up next to her.

"Hey, beautiful," said Harry, putting his arm around her stomach. "What are you thinking about?"

Sarah stood up straight as she continued to watch Bruce's fin knife across the black ocean surface. "I've been thinking about those people we met on the *Missouri* the other day."

"You mean the Ravocs? Those two were characters, weren't they?"

"Do you know what Natalia told me? She said that they were on their way to the Mexican Coast to retrieve some "more treasure" of theirs. Then she hesitated like she was hiding something."

"That's funny," said Harry. "Because Mister Ravoc said that they were on their way to Mexico as well. He was very hesitant to fill me in on any real details as to why." Harry stopped as a realization struck him.

"What is it?" Sarah asked.

Harry smiled. "I think that the Ravocs have discovered the lost treasure of Santa Anna."

A sinister smile spread across Sarah's face. "Are you thinking what I'm thinking?"

Harry followed her gaze as she looked down at Bruce's dorsal fin circling the inside of its pen, then looked at her again. "You're not."

Sarah shrugged. "We got away with it once. I mean, if Bruce could make Jason's death look like an accident he can do the same with the Ravocs. Right?"

Harry sighed. "But what do I tell Admiral Zanuck? He's about to take the fleet out on RIMPAC exercises. And I need his approval to let Bruce out of his cage."

"Just tell him whatever you need to tell him," said Sarah. "I'm sure you'll think of something. You're good at that." She kissed him gently on the lips. "Do this for us and I'll see to it that you personally get another reward from me, *personally*."

Harry smiled as he felt his spirits suddenly lifted and he moved his hand down her back. "Then perhaps I should get the shark ready to go."

"We've got until tomorrow," said Sarah. "No rush."

Harry and Sarah had no idea that their conversation was being recorded by a small hand-held dish which was wired to a voice-activated tape recorder attached to Natalia's waist. She wore a black wetsuit as she sat silently on a dark-colored jet ski in the total darkness, beyond the reach of the *Garage Sale's* lights. She listened to every word they uttered through headphones connected to the recorder.

Only after Harry and Sarah had disappeared inside did she put down the dish, gunned the jet ski's engine and raced back to their waiting yacht.

# 17

The thirty-foot long sailing yacht *Summer Dink* cut across the waves of the Pacific, her single triangle sail full with wind as the sleek vessel was pushed east toward Isla de Guadalupe. Her hull was red and polished so that sunlight gleamed off of it. On the bow next to the ship's name was its serial number: MS 15 LF.

On the bridge, Jason steered his new command toward its destination using a satellite compass, one of many devices given to him by Admiral Zanuck to help his plan work. The satellite phone that he kept nearby on the console began to make a tune. He answered it on the second ring. "Shaw. Yes, Admiral Zanuck. Two-hundred miles from Isla Guadalupe." Natalia walked onto the bridge as Jason continued to recieve updates from Zanuck. "They are? Understood. Yes, sir. I will. Thank you, Admiral."

Jason hung up. "Right on schedule."

"What is it?" Natalia asked.

Jason grinned as he turned the ship's wheel. "The *Squalas* just sailed from the *Garage Sale* and is following us east, with Bruce in tow."

"How does Admiral Zanuck know that? I though he was out at sea conducting RIMPAC exercises."

"He's keeping an eye on them with a satellite. He can watch their every move."

Natalia moved up next to her husband as he put his arm around her. "Jason, I have to admit that I'm a little nervous. I mean, Jacobs and Sarah have a great white shark as big as a whale under their control. Bruce could swallow us and our yacht whole. How are we suppose to beat them?"

It suddenly occurred to Jason that he had not filled her in on the rest of his plan. "Hold this for a minute," he said, allowing her to take the helm, then disappeared out of the bridge. He returned a moment later carrying a long secure suitcase and placed it on the console for her to see.

Jason turned the safe dials until he found the correct combination, then paused. He looked at his Russian wife. "What you are about to see is totally classified."

Natalia nodded. "I gathered as much."

Jason opened the case. Inside was a six-foot, torpedo-like object that reminded Natalia of a toy submarine.

"What is it?" Natalia asked, still holding the wheel.

"Our secret weapon," said Jason. "This is a remote control submersible that Harry and I used to maintain control of the chip inside of the shark's brain."

"Doesn't your former partner also have one of these?"

"Not quite. This one has a bonus installment inside of it, a jamming device that can fry the computer inside of Harry's mini-sub from a range of a hundred yards underwater, allowing us to gain control of Bruce."

Natalia smiled as she began to feel more relieved about Jason's plans. "Impressive." She returned to steering the yacht as Jason closed the case and kissed her on the cheek.

"There is nothing to worry about my love," said Jason. "Harry and Sarah don't know it yet, but they are about to become the hunted."

# 18

The twenty-foot rigid-hulled inflatable boat cut across the water off the coast of Northern Isla de Guadalupe, bouncing on the occasional wave as Sarah steered from the helm. Harry was busy monitoring the notepad computer that controlled the giant shark.

He had previously told Admiral Zanuck that he was taking Bruce out for a few days for some tests to update the mind-control technology in the shark. To Harry's amazment, Zanuck had fallen for the lie and gave him the authority to let the monster out of its cage.

For the past week they had been able to track the *Summer Dink* all the way down to the Mexican Coast while Bruce obediantly trailed the *Squalus* as it transmitted commands to the chip in his brain. Harry had planned to wait until the Ravocs had revealed the location of the treasure then send Bruce in to attack the sailing yacht and kill the Ravocs close to the island. From there they would salvage the treasure for themselves. The plan was foolproof.

"Stop here," said Harry.

Sarah cut their speed and walked up to her boyfriend as he stood poking at his computer screen. She noticed how he seemed confused and irritated as he typed commands that their giant pet, somewhere below the surface, seemed to ignore.

"Is something wrong?" asked Sarah.

Harry furiously poked his finger on the small screen. "Bruce isn't responding to any of my commands."

There was a blur of static on the screen. Harry slapped the side of the computer and the original view came back on. "It's almost like someone's jamming us."

"Where is Bruce now?" asked Sarah.

Harry pushed another button that showed a beeping red light on a satellite map of the island. "He's about nine-hundred feet down, and coming up fast. It looks like he's headed right for..." Harry trailed off. He turned to Sarah with a look of horror on his face like she had never seen before. "Sarah," he said. "Jump! Now!"

Harry and Sarah both turned and leaped out over opposite ends of the boat just as an enormous set of murderous jaws exploded out of the ocean beneath them. There was a loud pop and hiss of escaping air as Bruce closed his enormous mouth around the inflatable boat. His five-inch triangular teeth cut through the rubber boat like butter and crushed it, causing the small craft to instantly deflate in his slicing grasp. Then just as quickly as he had appeared Bruce slipped below the surface and was gone, taking the boat with him.

Sarah gasped for air as her head broke the surface. She looked around her, calling out for Harry but saw no sign of him. Instead, she saw the six-foot black dorsal fin and crescent tail as Bruce circled her. Sarah instantly became paralyzed with fear. This was it. She was about to die in the most unbareable way that she could imagine.

*Now I know what it must have felt like for Jason.*

Then Bruce whipped his tail up into the air and disappeared.

Something struck the water next to Sarah and she screamed, thinking that the shark had resurfaced next to her. She looked and realized that it was a float and followed the connecting line up to the boat that had thrown it. It was the *Summer Dink*. Natalia Ravoc stood waving on the bow.

Sarah wasn't exactly thrilled that the Ravocs had found out that they were so near their treasure hideout but it was better than swimming with Bruce. She wrapped her arms around the float and they pulled her up dripping wet onto the deck.

Harry was already there with a blanket draped over his shoulders and he gathered Sarah up into his arms as he helped Natalia pull the rope out of the water. Natalia put another blanket around Sarah as she stood shivering and her cheeks began to change color.

Natalia ran past her husband toward the galley to get something warm for them to drink. Joseph Ravoc stood for a moment with his hands on his hips as he watched both of them shake in each other's embrace, scared out of their minds.

"Well," said Jason, maintaining his disguise. "Doctor Jacobs. Miss Shaw. Fancy meeting you here."

The sky turned a crimson red as the sun began to set below the horizon. The *Summer Dink* and the *Squalas* both sat at anchor a short distance from each other on the calm, pond-like ocean as Harry and Jason walked on the deck discussing what had happened earlier that day.

"A whale shark?" said Jason in his Russian accent.

Harry nodded. He had manage to cover up his and Sarah's scheme by telling their rescuers that they had arrived off Mexico's shore on a routine patrol to monitor some new sonar equipment and that one of their tests had disturbed a whale shark as it passed beneath them.

"Well I'm not sure if that's what it was," said Jason, "but it certainly was the biggest thing that I've ever seen."

"You saw it?" Harry asked, suddenly alarmed.

"I thought I saw a tail splash out of the ocean but that's about it."

Harry felt relieved. If Bruce were to be reported to the media a second time like he was a year before, Admiral Zanuck would become enraged and probably even feed Harry to his own shark. "Well, thank you for helping us today, Mister Ravoc. We really appreciate it."

Harry extended his hand and Jason politelly shook it.

"My pleasure, Doctor."

Sarah and Natalia came up to join them. Harry put his arm around Sarah and said, "We probably should get going."

After saying their good byes Harry and Sarah boarded a boat that the Ravocs had loaned to them, started the motor and drove toward their yacht.

Later that night, as the two vessels became separated in the darkness, Jason picked up his satellite phone and contacted Admiral Zanuck.

"Admiral. The jammer on the new mini-sub works like a charm."

Sarah came out of the *Squalas's* bathroom dressed in a white cotten robe and a towel wrapped around her head.

"Okay," she told Harry. "Now that the mutual hogwash is anchored twelve miles away, tell me what the hell went wrong out there."

Harry ignored her as she came into the chart room to give him a piece of her mind. He already had the remote mini-sub propped up on a table. The cover on the top was open and he was working on the inside with his tools. As Sarah watched, he pulled up a pair of tweezers that held a small cube from inside the remote vehicle.

Sarah examined it closely. The cube appeared to be partially melted and burned.

"I found out what happened to Bruce," Harry said. "The computer inside the mini-sub has been fried. What you're looking at is the result of a top secret technology that's designed to short curcuit an enemy's computer and render them vulnerable to incoming attacks."

Sarah looked at him with concern. "What are you saying?"

"Whoever did this was able to get to our mini-sub in a way not easy to find."

"Are you saying that we were sabotaged?"

Harry nodded. "Someone doesn't want us out here."

"Well it still doesn't explain why Bruce attacked us." Sarah took the tweezers from Harry. She examined the burned computer chip with a sudden curiosity, wondering how it was even possible to effect something without ever touching it.

"Do you know what could've done this?" she asked.

"You're asking the wrong question," said Harry. "You and I are the only people still alive who know that this thing even exists. The question is: *who* could've done this?"

# 19

The next morning, Harry and Sarah set out in another inflatable navy raft to give their plan a second try. As before, Sarah steered the motorized raft from the control column while Harry guided their secret weapon with his computer notepad.

Harry had managed to replace the computer inside the mini-sub the night before. Now he was taking extra precautions, keeping an eye out for other vessels that may look suspicious and checking the sonar on the mini-sub for any further attempts of sabotage. Unlike soundwaves, electronic signals are difficult to transmit underwater. If whoever sabotaged the mini-sub the day before wanted to do so again they would have to come in close to the mini-sub to effectively overload it, more than enough time for the sonar to detect them and call in Bruce.

For the moment, however, Harry and Sarah seemed to have the open ocean all to themselves. The navy raft continued to bounce on the waves as they made their way toward the *Summer Dink*.

After arriving at their chosen ambush spot Sarah cut the engine and they waited.

Static suddenly appeared on the computer screen as Harry steered the mini-sub a hundred feet beneath their raft. Then the green light indicating the mini-sub's signal on the screen disappeared while the red light continued to blink as it moved closer to the raft.

The lifeless mini-sub surfaced right next to the inflatable boat. Harry and Sarah sat perfectly still as they watched the computer screen. Sarah slowly grabbed Harry's hand and squeezed it tight as the red light flashed across the map in their direction. Bruce was moving slowly this time and keeping his distance from the raft.

Harry raised his hand and pointed over to port. "He's about to come up over there," he whispered.

A few seconds after he said that the black dorsal fin surfaced just a few yards from where they floated. It cut through the water as Bruce began to circle the raft from beneath the surface. Harry and Sarah stared in frozen horror as the fin turned in front of them and silently came toward the raft. It passed close enough to them that Sarah could have easily reached out and touched it. The sixty-foot fish moving beneath them caused the inflatable boat to turn in the swirl of Bruce's movement. Then the fin sank out of sight and was gone.

Harry and Sarah stared at the spot where the shark had disappeared for a long moment, not sure if it was safe to move again. They both jumped as they suddenly heard a loud electronic beep right next to their boat. The mini-sub was working again, its flashing light and computer system functioning once more. Harry and Sarah exhaled a sigh of relief at the little submersible. Harry put his arm around Sarah as they both began to laugh.

"It must have been the new computer-"

Bruce's massive tail came up from underneath and catapulted the raft out of the water, sending its occupants flying straight up into the air. Sarah screamed as she was tossed end over end into the sky. Blue space and horizon spun out of control as she first went up then back down. She hit the ocean hard and her screams came out as bubbles as she suddenly found herself submerged underwater.

Bruce shot past underneath her, causing her to tumble end over end once again in the shark's current. Sarah realized that she had used up all of her air and that she needed to get back to the surface. But for a brief moment, she couldn't tell which way was up and she began to panic. Finally she saw the blot of light that she realized was the sun and she swam toward it.

After what seemed like an eternity Sarah sucked in air as her head cleared the surface. She turned around looking for Harry. The raft was upside down a few feet from her and she stroked to reach it.

"Sarah!" That was Harry's voice. He was behind her and treading water toward the upturned raft as well. That's when they saw the ship approaching.

The *Summer Dink* was bearing down on them, apparently having taken its load of treasure from the Ravoc's hiding place. Sarah grabbed onto a life preserver as it struck the water and she was hoisted up onto the deck, where she once again found herself face-to-face with Captain Ravoc. He looked at her in disbelief.

"That was no whale shark."


After recovering Harry, Sarah and their raft, Jason-still disguised as Captain Ravoc-had a serious conversation with both shark victims on the deck. Both of them were once again draped in towels and sipping cups of hot coffee, not wanting to say much. Jason felt satisfied that they now knew what it was like to be at the mercy of Bruce like he had been. But he wasn't finished with them yet, and for the moment he still had to play the part of the Russian explorer.

"Do either of you care to talk to me about what I saw today?" he asked them. "I would appreciate it if you were honest with me. If there's a giant man-eater on the loose don't you think people should know about it?"

"We can't let anyone know about it." All heads turned to Harry as he finally broke the silence. It didn't matter if they knew about Bruce anymore, he realized. The Ravocs still didn't know that they were controlling him and that still gave him and Sarah an advantage. If anything, this could lure the Ravocs out into the open where Bruce would be able to deal with them much more easily.

"That shark," Harry continued, "is government property. He's part of a top secret project that I'm not suppose to talk about."

"Let me guess," said Jason. "He escaped. And now you have to catch him and bring him back before he begins to attack public beaches."

Harry nodded. "Can you imagine what a sixty-foot long great white shark could do to a beach full of humans? Think about it."

Natalia put her hands over her mouth as she listened, pretending to be terrified by Harry's story.

Jason simply sat down in front of Harry and asked, "What can we do to help?"

Harry tried to act surprised by his offer. "Well, I'm not sure. I mean, I don't want to endanger you or your wife, Mister Ravoc."

Jason held up a hand to silence him. "I wouldn't be able to live with myself if I took no actions to stop that murderous beast from killing anyone. Just tell me what I can do."

"I'm not sure," said Harry. "How about we meet at a certain location tomorrow morning and we'll come up with a battleplan together?"

Jason stood with Harry and Sarah. "Very good. How about to the west of the island. Let's say ten o clock?"

"Sounds good," said Harry, and he shook his hand.


After returning to the *Squalas*, Sarah went to the bedroom and prepared to go to sleep. She was aware of Harry's presence as he came into the room.

"What was it this time?" she asked. "Did someone jam you again?"

"No," said Harry. "I think this time it was the replacement computer in the mini-sub. I probably should've tuned it a little better before we sent it out. I'll have it fixed tomorrow."

"I sure hope so."

Harry came up behind her and moved his hands around her waist toward her stomach. "How about you and me do something together to help us forget about the last two days, huh?"

Sarah pushed his hands away and spun around to face him. "Were we having these problems when we used the shark to kill Jason?"

"No."

"Did the mini-sub malfunction?"

"No."

"Did Bruce attack us?"

"No."

"Then why is all of that happening now?"

"Baby, sometimes these things happen. No one knows why."

"Well until Bruce has eaten the Ravocs, sunk their boat, and we have loaded their treasure onto our yacht, you will not be going to bed with me again. Now get it to work this time."

Harry held up his hands to make Sarah calm down.

*I can't believe that I fell in love with such a demanding wretch.*

"Okay," he said. "I'll have it working as good as new tomorrow morning. I promise. Goodnight."

Sarah allowed him to kiss her on the cheek and watched him walk out of the room.


Jason removed his fake beard and eye contacts. He studied his handsome face in the mirror. Satisfied that he had removed all of the disguises that made him Captain Joseph Ravoc, he prepared for bed. He dressed into his black T-shirt and gray pajama pants and sat on the bed waiting for his wife.

Natalia emerged from the yacht's bathroom a few moments later wearing only her black sleeveless undershirt and panties.

Jason thought that she was stunning. In his opinion she was the most beautiful woman alive. Her long, slim body was beautifully curved and long red hair flowed down her back. Her face revealed a woman who was not afraid to speak her mind and at the same time there was a kindness in the way that she looked at him that made Jason unable to resist her.

For Jason, Natalia was the greatest thing that had ever happened to him. He knew that she had gone through a lot of grief in her life. But instead of defeating her those hardships had made her stronger and enabled her to help Jason recover from his own traumatic experience.

He was madly in love with her.

In the year since they had first met Natalia had made Jason the happiest man on earth and he wanted nothing more than to make her as happy in their marriage as she had made him.

Jason watched as Natalia walked up to him and sat in his lap. She wrapped her arms around his neck and kissed him softly on the mouth.

"I love you," she said.

Jason looked into her deep blue eyes from only inches away. "I love you so much, Natalia. I have no idea what I would do without you."

They both moved forward and held onto each other in a loving embrace as they both found comfort in each other's arms. Jason kissed his wife's cheek as he put his hands around her slim form, not wanting to let go of her.

After a moment, Natalia gently pushed him back and looked into his eyes again.

"Jason, what are we doing? You've got enough evidence against them now to put them away forever. Why are we playing around? I just want to get this over with so that we can get on with our lives together."

Jason ran his fingers along Natalia's cheek as he moved some strands of hair from her face. "You're right. So do I. And I promise that I'll bring all of this to an end tomorrow."

"But why tomorrow? Why not end it now?"

Jason looked at her for a moment before he finally told her.

"Because tomorrow is the first anniversary of when they tried to kill me."

# 20

The next morning, Sarah came onto the bridge of the *Squalas* in her white robe. Harry was nowhere to be seen. He had apparently gone out to make sure that the shark was working this time.

She made herself a cup of coffee and took careful sips from it as she sat down in Harry's chair. She stood up again when she heard the ship's fax machine printing out a message. When it was finished she ripped off the piece of paper and read it:

Attention United States Naval Research Vessel Squalas: you are hereby ordered to proceed to the northwest out of Mexican territorial waters. The United States Coast Guard Cutter Firebolt is en route to take Harry Timothy Jacobs and Sarah Marie Shaw into custody for the murders of Benjamin Gardner, Tina Issacs and Susan Backline.

The message and the coffee cup both dropped from Sarah's hands as she saw her whole life collapse right before her eyes. She felt her heart begin to race in her chest as she stood in stunned terror on the bridge, taking deep breaths to calm herself.

"Oh dear God," she said over and over. "This is not happening. This is not happening. This is just a bad dream."

After a moment, Sarah realized that she needed to get ahold of Harry. Maybe he could think of something, sail for a Mexican port and then disappear, use Bruce to attack any Coast Guard ships that came after them. Anything to avoid prison.

She ran for the ship's console, picked up the radio, then hesitated. Something wasn't right. She picked up the message from the coffee-stained floor and read it again. They had been charged with the murders of the other three people on the *Amity*, but there was no mention of Jason himself. Why?

Sarah jumped as she heard three knocks behind her. She spun around and gaped at the man whom she had previously taken to be a Russian treasure hunter standing in the doorway. Now she was looking at a family member who she had never expected to see alive again. Jason flashed a white-toothed smile at Sarah.

"Happy Fourth of July, little sister."

A few miles out to sea, Harry Jacobs stood at the controls of the rigid-hulled inflatable boat, his eyes focused on the computer notepad in his hand. He poked at the screen and the mini-sub sped across the water and became submerged. This time Harry was determined to make the device work so that Bruce could make a flawless attack on the Ravocs' ship the next day. He had no intention of returning to the *Squalas* that evening until he was certain that Bruce would obey his every command like he did a year earlier when he had used it to kill Jason Shaw and his friends.

The red light on the sub began flashing as it maneuvered beneath the surface, with Bruce following about twenty yards behind. For the first time in two days Harry was pleased as the shark responded perfectly to his commands. But what Harry did not know was that a few yards away Natalia Shaw was under the water guiding her husband's own mini-sub by remote control toward Harry's machine as Jason had done the previous two days.

This time, however, her sub carried a small barrel-shaped explosive device connected to a long rod on the sub's nose.

Jason had told Natalia the night before that he was going to confront Sarah the next morning and had asked her to use his mini-sub to take out Harry's remote vehicle by placing the explosive on his sub. This would easily allow Natalia to then use her sub to gain control of Bruce and command him to encircle Harry until the Coast Guard arrived.

As she steered the remote vehicle through the water toward Harry's torpedo-shaped machine, Natalia knew exactly how to carry out her assignment. She was to press the rod on her sub's nose against the side of Harry's sub. The magnet on the small explosive would then connect to the metal hull. A long string connected to Natalia's sub would then activate the detonator and destroy Harry's machine once the two subs were at a safe distance from each other.

At first the plan of attack seemed to be going as it was suppose to be. Natalia carefully pressed the explosive against Harry's sub and the magnet connected to its hull. But at that same moment Harry turned his sub to the right.

The mini-sub's propeller became entangled in the line connected to the explosive which also sucked in Natalia's sub. The line became taught as both machines were pulled into each other and the detonator was activated.

Sarah found herself unable to speak as Jason stepped onto the bridge. She stared wide-eyed at him like she was facing a ghost. "Jason," she finally managed. "I thought you were dead."

Jason began to walk toward her as he talked. "I was dead. When I saw Bruce murder my friends right in front of my eyes, and realized later that my one and only sister was the brains of the plot to end my life, I did die. But somewhere over the past year that followed, as I traveled across the Pacific with a woman who *wanted* me alive, I found a reason to live again. And that I needed to survive to avenge the friends that you had taken from me."

Sarah walked backwards as Jason approached, only to stop when she felt the chair behind her. Her life was over. She knew it. And she began to cry. "What do you want me to say?"

Jason marched right up to her. Sarah quickly sat down in the seat as he put his hands on the armrests and brought his face right up to hers. "What I want," he said, "is to know what on earth it was that I did to make my own flesh and blood want to murder me so badly."

The bomb detonated underwater like a small depth charge. Harry almost jumped out of his raft as a geyser of white spray exploded upward just a few yards from him. He checked his notepad computer.

Beneath the surface, Bruce, finally free from his master's control over his very mind, instantly dove straight down into the depths, then began to rise once again.

Harry watched in horror on his notepad computer as the red dot began to move up the west side of the island directly toward the *Squalas*.


Sarah had no idea what to tell her brother as he stared at her face to face like he was ready to rip her throat out. "Look," she said. "Jason, please. We can find a way to settle this."

"It's too late for that, Sarah," Jason told her. "I've already given Admiral Zanuck all the evidence that he needs to put you and Harry away for the rest of your days. But before you go tell me what it was that made you want to kill me."

Sarah opened her mouth to tell him the truth but was unable to. She bowed her head in sorrow, realizing that nothing she could say would fix her predicament.

"It was Dad's fortune, wasn't it?" said Jason, standing up straight. "When he gave me a bigger share than he gave to you it made you mad. It didn't matter that you got a big share of your own. You wanted the whole package. I'll bet that's why you began to date Harry, so that you could romance him into using our shark to kill me. That was it, wasn't it? I'll bet you were planning to kill him off someday as well so that you could have all of Dad's money to yourself. It all makes sense now. You've always been a selfish, spoiled rotten wretch with zero empathy toward others that only saw me as an embaressment to you and your perfect little life. You felt like Dad and Mom favored me over you somehow. And once I was finally dead you could live a trouble free life now that you didn't have a sibling to share everything with."

Jason had to fight the urge to cry as he yelled at Sarah. He did not enjoy talking to his sister like this. Despite what she had done to him, what she had wanted to do to him, he still loved her.

He knelt down in front of her as Sarah put her face in her hands. Jason grabbed onto her hands as Sarah looked at him with blood shot eyes.

"This is not easy for me either."

Suddenly Harry Jacobs' voice came over the yacht's radio. "Sarah. Baby, wake up. You need to get off the yacht right now, Sweetie. I've lost control of Bruce and he's headed right for you. Please tell me you're awake."

Sarah, suddenly alarmed, looked at her brother for approval to evacuate. Jason pointed her back into her chair as he walked to the bridge console. He picked up the radio and spoke into it. "Do you believe in ghosts, Harry?"

There was a silence. "Jason?"

Jason grinned. He had been wanting to surprise Harry since he had first sent Bruce to kill him, although he had been hoping to do it in person.

At that moment a tremendous force like the impact of a freight train struck the *Squalas*, knocking Jason and Sarah across the room. Sarah began to panic as Jason grabbed her arm and pulled her onto her feet.

"We need to get to the helicopter."

Sarah wrestled her hand out of his. "No. You said it yourself, Jason. I'm going to jail for the rest of my days anyway. I might as well stay here."

"Don't talk like that," said Jason. "Once Bruce pulls this ship down you won't stand a chance against him."

"You survived him."

Jason grabbed her shoulders and looked her in the eyes. "I am not going to leave you here at the mercy of that animal like you did to me."

Sarah suddenly realized that her brother's motive all this time was not revenge against her. Despite the fact that she had tried to kill him he was still concerned for her safety.

Finally, after making up her mind, she nodded and they both took off running for the helipad on the stern.


Harry sat in his inflatable raft, desparately trying to reach Sarah. Was that really Jason? How was he still alive?

"Sarah? Baby, pick up the radio. Please somebody say something."

As he tried to reach the *Squalas*, Harry heard the sound of a ship motor coming up behind him. He turned around. The *Summer Dink* came up alongside his raft and stopped.

Natalia Ravoc came out onto the deck dripping wet in her red bikini. She smiled at Harry as she leaned over the rail and held up a pair of electric cords connected to a small propeller and round head on either ends.

"You should really keep a tighter leash on your pet, Doctor Jacobs," said Natalia as she tossed the device into the raft in front of him.

Harry looked at it closely, and realized that it was the remains of Bruce's mini-sub. The sound of a chambering firearm made him pause. He slowly looked back up and saw the Russian woman pointing a 1911 Colt pistol directly at him.

Natalia smiled. "Now get on board."

By the time Jason and Sarah came out onto the helipad deck on the stern the *Squalas* was already beginning to lean over onto its port side.

Jason jumped into the pilot seat of the helicopter and buckled up his sister in the passenger seat next to him. He didn't bother to put on the radio headset that was required for all navy helicopter pilots and quickly flipped on the many switches that started the copter's rotor blades.

Neither Jason or Sarah bothered to say anything to each other, never offered any words of sorrow as the blades spun and the small craft lifted into the air. All that mattered at that moment was their own survival.

The copter had just lifted off the tilting helipad when the *Squalas* was hit hard once again. Bruce rammed his head hard into the yacht like a battering ram and nearly lifted the vessel out of the water. As the helicopter hovered over the scene, Jason and Sarah watched in amazement as the giant shark pushed the entire vessel sideways.

Bruce's black upper body was visible above the surface as he furiously thrashed his tail back and forth, his snout pushing deeper into the gaping wound that he had made in the yacht's hull. Jason had forgotten just how big his shark really was. At sixty feet in length he was nearly one-third the size of the *Squalas*.

After a moment Bruce suddenly stopped as he became aware of a new target hovering less than fifty feet above him. The shark pulled its nose out of the massive hole in the ship's side, allowing water to pour in, then dived straight down into the deep.

Jason watched Bruce throw his tail up and then vanish beneath the surface before turning the copter toward the south. He would need to send out a mayday to all ships in the area. Admiral Zanuck would ring his neck for letting Bruce escape again but that was a matter for another time. Right now he just needed to find a way to hunt down his creation and destroy it before it could do anymore harm.

Harry sat down uncomfortably on the hot deck of the *Summer Dink*. His hands were held in place above his head by a pair of handcuffs chained around the ship's metal railing.

Natalia stood with her arms folded a few paces in front of him. She fixed the navy scientest with a hard-eyed stare as she watched his every move, the pistol firmly in her right hand.

Harry looked up at the tanned, red-haired beauty that had just taken him prisoner as she stood wet and dripping in front of him. He decided to enjoy the view while he could. It would be a long time before he would ever see such a beautiful woman like this again.

"So you're Jason's wife?" Harry asked.

"That is correct," said Natalia. Harry looked her up and down and asked, "Well where on earth did he find a hot thing like you?"

Natalia suddenly became angry and pointed the pistol at his face. "We found each other, you pervert. And you would do well to exercise your right to remain silent."

At that moment she noticed a helicopter in the distance. It was flying low over the water and headed toward the *Summer Dink* at top speed. Somehow Natalia knew that Jason was on board that aircraft as it flew toward her. That was when she also noticed something else in the water beneath the copter. She looked down at Harry. "You will stay exactly where you are!"

Harry suddenly became alarmed as she ran toward him. "Wait a minute! Hey!"

Natalia ignored his cries as she stepped over him onto the iron rails and leaped forward into the ocean, leaving Harry alone to suffer beneath the hot scorching sun.

It wasn't until they were halfway to the *Summer Dink* that it occurred to Jason to put on the radio headset in the helicopter. He began radioing to any US warships in the area.

"Mayday! Mayday! This is Jason Shaw of the United States Navy. Does anyone copy, over?"

Suddenly the enormous shark's upper torso rose out of the sea. Bruce bit down on the landing strut, the aluminum bending in his clenching teeth. Sarah screamed as Jason wrestled against the joystick with both hands. The enormous shark began to drag the outmatched copter from the sky.

Jason reacted quickly, throwing the joystick over onto one side and causing the helicopter to flip over onto its back. The spinning helicopter blades cut into the shark's thick hide behind its head, sending pieces of flesh and metal flying in every direction. The destroyed blades were still spinning as Bruce, Jason, Sarah, and the copter all fell down into the sea.

Jason was blasted by a wall of water that filled the cabin within seconds. He fumbled desparately to unlock Sarah's seat belt buckle while his sister panicked and the cabin began to roll end over end.

He then felt his own seat belt come loose off of his shoulders. Jason turned his head to look just as Natalia leaned out across the cabin in front of him and cut Sarah's shoulder straps with a diver's knife. Jason then quickly pulled Sarah out of the sinking machine, put his arms around both women's waists and all three of them began to swim up toward the surface.

The decapitated Bruce began to sink to the bottom along with the demolished helicopter, its severed torso unleashing a thick red cloud of blood as it descended into the deep. Then the aluminum frame of the helicopter groaned, making a sound like a growling dinosaur as both it and the dead shark faded from view into the dark abyss below.

Jason, Sarah and Natalia gasped for air as their heads surfaced among the bubbling crimson water. Jason spat sea water out of his mouth as Natalia swam up to him. They both laughed as Natalia wrapped her arms around her husband's neck and pressed her forehead against his.

As he embraced her and looked into his wife's deep, beautiful eyes, Jason realized how blessed he was to have Natalia as his own. From the moment they had first met she had saved his life in more ways than he could ever hope to repay her for. Jason and Natalia stopped laughing and each one looked into the other's eyes as they both realized how much they had both come to need each other. Jason now knew more than ever that he could not go on in life without Natalia and promised himself that he would never take her for granted ever.

"Thank you," said Jason, "for saving my life."

Natalia said nothing as she pulled herself in close to him and pressed her body against his as they both held onto each other tight.

Sarah floated by herself in her life jacket as she watched her brother and sister-in-law embrace in the water. "Jason," she said. "I want you to know that you were wrong. There was a part of me that did feel guilty about what I did to you."

Jason looked at her for a moment. "But that wasn't enough to stop you, was it?"

Sarah turned away as a tear fell down her face. "I'm sorry."

Realizing that there was nothing more that he could say to help his sister, Jason turned back to his wife. Natalia looked past his shoulder and nodded at something behind him.

"Here comes your boss."

Jason turned around and saw the white-hulled coast guard cutter in the distance knifing through the water toward them. He could feel his wife put her arms around his shoulders as she rested her head next to his.

"You know, I use to be so afraid of the water."

**Natalia smiled. "I can't imagine why."**

Manufactured by Amazon.ca
Bolton, ON

33323266R00068